Praise for *New York 1, Tel Avi*

"Reading *New York 1, Tel Aviv 0* is lik
port stamps—it's your ticket to the uncharted worlds of the most fraught and fascinating characters in contemporary fiction. Shelly Oria's writing has everything: insights that will grab you by the throat; a voice that's wholly, disarmingly original; and a heart that fills and throbs and bursts. These stories will astonish you." **—Diana Spechler, author of *Who by Fire* and *Skinny***

"Fierce, funny, and utterly captivating, every story in this superb collection rings with aching truth about our strange, sad world and all the wonder and beauty there is to behold within it. By turns tender and provocative, Shelly Oria writes with great compassion and stunning grace about fear and failure, loss and longing, isolation and intimacy." **—Aryn Kyle, author of *Boys and Girls Like You and Me* and *The God of Animals***

"Shelly Oria's gorgeous stories pass over and through borders between nations, genders, and bodies, all the while fully aware of the contradictions contemporary culture presents."
—Samantha Hunt, author of *The Invention of Everything Else*

"Trying to figure out what an Israeli is, who an Israeli is in America, who the ones are who go back and forth, the devastatingly observant Shelly Oria takes us to Brooklyn and Manhattan, Tel Aviv and Jerusalem, and, in one of the most memorable of these stories, Albany! Searching to describe her tone, her laugh-out-loud originality, and her (mostly young) deliciously mixed-up, love-addicted, often-rueful characters, I'd say fresh—yes, fresh as the brilliant shock of new paint." **—Honor Moore, author of *The Bishop's Daughter***

"How can a voice be so direct and yet so delicate? In *New York 1, Tel Aviv 0*, Shelly Oria tenderly lays out the truth about human beings, creatures so intelligent they are able to outwit themselves most of the time. Oria's stories also reveal the rare moments when we humans find ourselves on the verge of transcendent revelation. But the heart of Oria's gift is her language: seductive, precise, and—over and over—startlingly beautiful." **—Nelly Reifler, author of *Elect H. Mouse State Judge***

"Shelly Oria has written a fiercely original, sharp and stunning collection. *New York 1, Tel Aviv 0* perfectly illuminates the breadth of life's complexities, is insightful throughout, and is funny when you least expect it."

—Alison Espach, author of *The Adults*

"In *New York 1, Tel Aviv 0*, Shelly Oria shows us the parts of ourselves that we most fear. And by rendering their brokenness, loneliness, and magic so tenderly, she shows us how to be tender. With her unflinching gaze, she shows us how to see." **—Melissa Febos, author of *Whip Smart***

"Whether in cooking classes or eye clinics or blood banks or fitting rooms, whether amidst time stoppages or amidst sounds that only one person can hear, Shelly Oria's characters are utterly original. *New York 1, Tel Aviv 0* is wondrous, wise, a dazzling debut."

—Joshua Henkin, author of *The World Without You*

"With their dark honesty, these are stories tuned in to the endless and extravagant strangeness of the world. Shelly Oria has a wonderful range of methods for dazzling us, and *New York 1, Tel Aviv 0* marks the arrival of a wildly talented writer." **—Joan Silber, author of *Ideas of Heaven***

NEW YORK 1, TEL AVIV 0

NEW YORK I,

STORIES

TEL AVIV O

SHELLY ORIA

FARRAR, STRAUS AND GIROUX NEW YORK

Farrar, Straus and Giroux
18 West 18th Street, New York 10011

Printed in the United States of America
First edition, 2014

These stories previously appeared, in slightly different form, in the following publications: *Brooklyn the Borough* ("Documentation," "Maybe in a Different Time" as "The Final Straw," "Tzfirah"), *Cream City Review* ("This Way I Don't Have to Be"), *Electric Literature's Recommended Reading* ("Phonetic Masterpieces of Absurdity"), *The Fiddleback* ("That Night"), *Indiana Review* ("New York 1, Tel Aviv 0"), *LIT* ("Victor, Changed Man"), *McSweeney's* ("The Beginning of a Plan"), *The Paris Review* ("My Wife in Converse"), *Quarterly West* ("We, the Women"), *Tinhouse.com* ("The Thing About Sophia"), *TriQuarterly* ("The Disneyland of Albany"), and *Spectrum* ("Beep").

Library of Congress Cataloging-in-Publication Data
Oria, Shelly, 1978–
[Short stories. Selections]
New York 1, Tel Aviv 0 : stories / Shelly Oria.
pages cm
ISBN 978-0-374-53457-8 (paperback) — ISBN 978-0-374-71175-7 (ebook)
I. Title. II. Title: New York one, Tel Aviv zero.

PS3615.R43 A6 2014
813'.6—dc23

2014017441

Designed by Abby Kagan

www.fsgbooks.com
www.twitter.com/fsgbooks • www.facebook.com/fsgbooks

10 9 8 7 6 5 4 3 2 1

For Nehama Segalovitz

CONTENTS

NEW YORK 1, TEL AVIV 0

NEW YORK 1, TEL AVIV 0

Saturday comes, and Zoë and I go to see Keith Buckley read in Soho. It is April and Manhattan and this is what I think about the air: it is crisp. I keep thinking: Crisp. I fantasize about taking a big bite and chewing the air, making obscenely loud noises as if the air on this island were a gum, or worse: sunflower seeds. While I'm thinking this, Zoë is being beautiful. She says, I'm so happy it's not cold anymore. She's wearing the purple halter top that Ron bought her for our one-year anniversary; I got *The Secrets of Mediterranean Cooking* because Ron thinks that I should open my own restaurant instead of wasting my talent in somebody else's kitchen. Zoë's halter top ties behind her neck, except every few minutes it gets loose, and I need to tie it again for her. It's too tight, she says every time, tugging on the knot.

At the bookstore, Zoë leads the way to her favorite

spot, third row center. Keith isn't here yet, she tells me without even looking around. How do you know? I ask, and she says, I need you to tie me up again, her eyes smiling, teasing. Then she asks, Has he ever read here before? I don't think so, I say, but I get confused between all the stores sometimes. Zoë says, I'm having the worst déjà vu; I feel like this moment already happened. I want to say, maybe it did; I've always felt that the present is just one way of looking at things. But these are thoughts I keep to myself, because I can't afford to lose Zoë. If I lose Zoë, Ron might go with her, and then I'd be completely alone in this city.

Zoë is the kind of person you lose easily: this has happened to many people. She's also the kind of person who will freak out when someone suggests there is more than one reality, then blame that someone for her freak-out. Once, after a Keith Buckley reading in Midtown, we sat on a bench, our backs to Central Park. I had moved from Tel Aviv only a few months earlier; Zoë was explaining how the park had been created in the 1850s. The idea of having a designated area for greenery struck me as odd; Tel Aviv isn't carefully planned like that—trees often choose their own location, and most streets stretch in unpredictable directions, creating a pattern of impulse.

We were waiting for Ron, and it was getting dark. Looking up and down, I noticed how this city, spreading to the sky, makes people smaller and faster. I was having one of my funny moods, when everything feels like a dream. I turned to Zoë and said, What if we're not real? What if we're just imagining this scene, right now, on this bench? Or what if somebody else is imagining us, and we are characters in this person's hallucination? I didn't know Zoë very well yet. I expected her to say I was crazy, or ask what the hell I was talking about. But she started shaking: first her knees, then her arms, then her entire body. She said, Don't fuck with my mind like that. I didn't know what to do. I put my hand on her knee and said, I'm here. Then I said, I'm real. She calmed down, but for the rest of the evening she kept saying, Don't ever fuck with me like that.

So, if you want Zoë to like you, you need to: (1) be a flexible, spontaneous person, because Zoë hates to wait but also hates to plan in advance; (2) love all literary events where Keith Buckley is reading; and (3) learn never to fuck with her mind.

In Israel, this is what you do when you enter a bar, a movie theater, a mall: you open your bag. You let the security guard look through your personal belongings, until he decides you're probably not carrying a bomb. The security guard is almost always a man. Sometimes he'll be thorough, like he knows something you don't; he might even use a metal detector that beeps if the interior of your jacket is explosive. But usually he'll just tap the bottom of the bag and signal with his eyes Go in. If you're a beautiful woman, you're likely to hear some kind of comment that acknowledges your beauty. Then you're free to roam whatever space it is, calm and confident, because in Tel Aviv, if you drink or eat or party enough, even the worst kind of war feels like peace.

When I first moved to New York, I kept opening my purse every time I entered a building, before realizing that there was no security guard. And every time I felt relieved, and every time I felt orphaned, and every time I felt surprised at both; there is a sense of comfort that you get when someone else is in charge of your safety, and I didn't yet know that in America danger is something you can choose to ignore.

Back then, I was subletting a tiny studio in Hell's Kitchen that had only one window. The building had a live-in super with a thick Romanian accent who treated me like his protégée because he was the Veteran Immigrant. My first day in the building, he said, Twelve years I live here now; it is like home. His accent was so thick that it took a few seconds of tossing the sounds in my brain to decipher their message, but I felt comforted. Then, three weeks later, he came over and said, New mall only few blocks from here; very expensive but you should go, look in the windows. I said I would, and I did. At the new Time Warner Center, I was going in as Ron was coming out. I reached to open my purse, and saw him smile, his Israeli radar letting me know I was busted. He seemed familiar, and happy; I stopped. We spent ten minutes trying to figure out where we knew each other from. The army? No, he left before he was eighteen, never served; the Peace Now rally in D.C.? No, I knew nothing about it; after a while, we gave up.

Zoë wants to step outside to smoke. We leave our coats and grab our bags. There is intimacy between us and a wide-shouldered guy with dreadlocks as we are squeezing our way out. Dreadlocks looks up at Zoë's shirt and Zoë says, Keep an eye on our stuff, okay? as if this is our friend and that's the least he can do. Dreadlocks nods; I can see inside his mind, very briefly, and it is full of one word: boobs.

Outside on Crosby Street, optimistic people believe that seats for this event are in abundance, so they just stand there, smoking or chatting. Zoë bums a cigarette from a pale baby-faced guy who looks familiar. I hear her say, No you don't get my number in return, and then a second later, You get . . . my gratitude, and then laughter. They are equidistant from me, but she is louder and I hear only her. Zoë never has cigarettes because she's quit smoking, so she always has to bum from people who haven't quit smoking yet. These people are usually around, though, and always into helping Zoë, so there's no reason to change the MO. Unless you count Ron as a reason; every time he smells cigarettes on Zoë's breath he squints and says, You need to *commit* to your health, Zoë, not just *talk* about it.

In Tel Aviv, walking into a bar is like stepping into a cloud. If you spend more than an hour inside the cloud, scent molecules get under your hair and skin, and they often take their time getting out. When you get back from the bar, if you don't want to inhale smoke from the pillow in your sleep, you head straight to the shower and turn the faucet all the way to red until the small room fills with steam. When I'm in Tel Aviv, I usually think, No big deal; then I get back to New York and feel indebted to the non-yellow walls, the guarantee of nicotine-free air once you walk into a room. It is true that in New York when you wash your clothes the water turns gray; you scrub, and inside the bubbles you see soot. But I don't mind it; I know that this urban dirt is the side effect of speed and productivity. I think: New York 1, Tel Aviv 0. It's an ongoing competition, a game that Ron and I invented, but I forget to keep track, so I have to start counting all over again every time.

Zoë is standing across from me smoking fast like she has to go somewhere and the cigarette is holding her back. I say, There's still plenty of time, you know. Zoë says, I might go with this guy for a drink. I give her a look. She says, Nothing serious, and looks away. I say, I think he used to work at the restaurant. Zoë pretends not to hear me, or maybe she really doesn't. Don't worry, I'll be back in time for Keith, she says; he's reading last. I think: As if that's the problem.

Zoë believes that no one understands Keith Buckley's work like she does, and that referring to him by his first name makes this fact clear. The truth is that no one understands Keith Buckley's work, not even Keith Buckley, if you ask me. But if I said that to Zoë—if I said, People laugh and shout and do the voices and download the ringtones because they want *to belong*; if I said, Zoë, think about it, Keith Buckley the phenomenon has very little to do with Keith Buckley the man—Zoë *wouldn't* think about it, not even just to pretend. Instead, she'd say, You don't have to go with me to these things, you know, and I would feel like our life is a reality show and I've just been voted off.

Don't tell Ron, Zoë says, putting out her cigarette, her eyes canvassing the sidewalk in search of pale guy. She steps on the butt and pulls me close; I hate the smell of smoking, but mixed with Zoë's breath it's all right. Love you, she says, and then kisses me, her tongue a tiny butterfly tapping mine; then she's gone.

I go back inside and think: What if I went home and took her jacket with me? By the time she came back, our seats would be taken and she'd have to watch Keith standing up, pushed against strangers who were too late. In Zoë's world, that's not an option. Or what if I did tell Ron? Would he confront her? Would things between the three of us change? I put my coat on my lap and tap my fleece-covered knee, because I feel like people can see my thoughts, and my thoughts are horrible. Since I can sometimes see people's thoughts a little bit, it's hard to remember that this is not the norm. Often, when thinking something new in a public place, I feel exposed.

When the reading starts, Dreadlocks turns to me and says, Where's your friend? She'll be back for Keith Buckley, I say. He nods slowly and seems to be saying, I'm glad we had this talk. He raises his right hand, which is holding a plastic cup. You want some coffee? he asks. No thanks, I say. He nods again. Let me know if you change your mind, he says, like there's something very important at stake.

When I see Zoë pushing through backs and arms to reach me, I regret not being invisible. I would pay a lot to see the look in her eyes if she returned and I weren't here, because I can't possibly imagine it. I have a good imagination, but with Zoë, the only way to know things is to see them. A man hisses Bitch as her elbow meets his abdomen, but she doesn't notice. When she sits down she is all excited, and smells of weed. Dreadlocks leans over and whispers, Your friend was very lonely without you. Zoë ignores him. Did you have a good time with the busboy? I ask. He's a bartender now, she says. A few seconds later, she puts her head on my shoulder. This is what I think: Greedy. A woman who can't stay faithful to two people will never know true satisfaction. Greedy, greedy, greedy. But this thought doesn't make me feel better.

Of course, to know Zoë is to know that she can never stay faithful to two people, or twelve, or twenty. But this is what I've learned today: there's knowing, and then there's *knowing*, and after the second kind comes seeing. The first kind of knowing is where Ron is: he knows that there must be other people, but he still chooses not to know. This is what you do when you don't want to know what you know: (1) You don't ask too many questions. (2) When you hear the two women you love giggle or whisper, you go to a different room and you tell yourself it's a choice, your choice, to give them privacy; you tell yourself that women often whisper, and it doesn't mean one of them is having sex with people you don't know. (3) When you smell another man on one of the women you love, you suggest we all hop in the shower; you say you feel sticky. When the same woman says, But I don't feel sticky, you say, Do it for me, then—in a way that tells her a shower is easier than a conversation.

The second kind of knowing happens when someone you love actually tells you what you already know. Often, for Zoë and me, this happens around evening time. In the bedroom that the three of us share, Zoë and I will be lying on top of our blanket—me, in my baggy Basic Training T-shirt that I use as pajamas; she, still all dressed up and smelling like the outside world, because she is always waiting for one of us to undress her. Zoë's hand under my T-shirt, up and down and tickling a little, she'll suddenly get a playful look in her eyes, stretching herself so that her lips face my ear. I fucked Randy the produce guy, she'll whisper to me and giggle, and then, Your skin is the softest I've ever touched—like Randy the produce guy has nothing to do with us.

So the second kind of knowing happens when you hear the woman you love whisper tales of other lovers in your ear, and sadness feels like something you swallowed without chewing, but the next morning it feels more like a bedtime story you listened to half asleep, something unworthy of your daytime attention.

And then there's seeing. Seeing happens when there's a

pale guy who looks harmless but he's not, and Zoë leaves you alone in a bookstore and comes back smelling of him. Seeing happens when you realize that you will never again be able to excite her like that, because the glow of her skin is about one thing: touching a new body.

Keith Buckley has a different voice for each character, as always; his stories are all dialogue, like a play, and very hard to follow (unless you've memorized them, and some of his fans have). Every time Keith Buckley says a character's name, the crowd shouts it back at him. Pinkers, Dire, Level. On the website you can download popular one-liners for your cell phone, even send a message to a friend using a character's voice. With every roar, Keith Buckley pauses, gives a slow blink that tries to look like gratitude. He clearly wants to appear humble, like he can't help but think, *How fortunate am I, how very, very fortunate.* But there's something about him that's plastic—fake and temporary. Every time he blinks, I think he might dissolve suddenly, but he never does.

Zoë laughs in all the right places, her laughter like a marble rolling down a slope. I can see her mind for about three seconds: she wants to mesmerize Keith Buckley with the sound of her laughter, the glitter of her bright green eyes. When the reading ends, Zoë turns around to look at the audience cheering; that's what she always does. Through the clatter of clapping hands, I hear her voice: He's such a . . . performer, you know? I know. I also know that all of a sudden she's sad. It doesn't take much with her. Well, do you want to buy the book again and have him sign it? I ask. Zoë has three signed copies of *Meadows of Fortitude*, Buckley's latest WebBook. She seems hesitant, and while waiting for her decision, this is what I think: We look like two friends at a lit event, not like two-thirds of a three-way couple. I think: It's fucked up; it's all fucked up. I try to smile at Zoë anyway, but my lips feel stiff.

Zoë shakes her head no, slowly. She says, I think we should just go. This is an important step for her; every time she approaches Keith Buckley, she thinks he must remember her by now, and the next thing that happens is disappointment. I say, Okay, let's go, and I can see so much air leaving her body at once, as if she were a pop-up doll deflating. Then it takes us almost ten minutes to get to the door because of all the people. Behind us someone says, Only in New York fucking City this many people show up to hear some bearded old dude make funny voices. A disgruntled snort follows, and I see Zoë wanting to turn around and respond, defend her Keith, but she just shrugs and looks at me with sad eyes that say, The things I want the most are the things I'll never have. This is what I feel like: a consolation prize.

We're practically out when Zoë says, I need to go to the bathroom. It's okay, I tell her. It's not okay, though, because bathroom of course means Keith Buckley. It's also not okay that whenever Ron isn't around, something shifts between us and she says things like *I need to go to the bathroom* when she means *I can't leave without trying to talk to Keith.* I want to say, I'll wait outside then, but instead I say, Want me to go with you?

This is why I moved to New York: I didn't want to go to India. Or South America, or Australia. In Israel, this is what you do when the IDF gives you your freedom back: you work and save money for about a year, and then go backpacking in a place cheap enough to host you for a long time. I was on that track just like everyone else, but when it was time to go, I realized that I never cared much for India and that the friend I was supposed to travel with, a gay guy named Yoni, was actually not completely gay and possibly in love with me. I was not in love with Yoni and not in love with India, but staying in Tel Aviv meant starting my life, or at least going to school. It's a scary thing, starting your life. So I signed up for cooking classes and flew to Manhattan, because that's where they were.

Keith Buckley is signing his WebBook and looking at Zoë like he can't quite place her. He seems troubled. Zoë is oddly quiet, standing still and waiting. Then Keith Buckley stops moving his pen, looks up once again, stares at Zoë. Something is happening, but I don't know what. I look at Zoë; if she has any answers, she's keeping them to herself. Keith Buckley says, I'm sorry, I have to ask; are you . . . ? Is that you? Zoë's voice is flat when she says, Am I who? I can see that Keith Buckley needs to take a deep breath, but he doesn't. Have you been stalking me? he asks. No, Zoë says quietly. Keith Buckley doesn't know what to do with her answer. She looks him straight in the eye and repeats, No. Inside my left ear, someone is scratching a chalkboard with long nails. Finally, Keith Buckley stops staring at Zoë, adds "uck" to his "Best of L," and she grabs the book, turns around. I follow Zoë's back out of the store, and it doesn't take as long this time. Her shoulder blades are sharp like they have some protecting to do. I feel an urge to touch them, as if they will soften when I do, and we will leave the store transformed, having learned something together.

When we step outside, we see Ron waiting for us. Zoë isn't happy to see him, and her upper lip tightens. My favorite girls, he says, and hugs us both, a three-way, end-of-the-week hug. He smells like he's already been home and taken a shower, and his scent calms me down. I cling to him and kiss his neck. For a few seconds, I feel hopeful, like maybe now we can double-click and delete, start the evening over. Zoë finds her way out of our hug and says, I'm not going home now. She sounds like a rebellious teenager. Daddy Ron says, Who said anything about going home? I thought we'd go out. Zoë says, Well I'm meeting someone. Then she quietly adds, A friend. She looks at me for help, but I look away, I look down. I see a cigarette butt on the concrete and wonder if it's Zoë's butt from before. Ron says, Zo, we said something about Saturday nights, remember?

Three weeks ago, we went out and saw a movie about a strikingly short ten-year-old boy who wants to make it to the NBA. He doesn't, but by the end of the film he's living on a farm, growing tomatoes and looking content. It was a bad movie that put us in a good mood. On the way home, I had my left hand in Zoë's back pocket while Ron held my right one, and I felt like I do on steamy days when I step into the big refrigerator at the restaurant. An hour later, we were sitting on cushions in our living room, playing poker and drinking wine, and Ron started mimicking the short boy's voice at thirteen, squeaky and whiny with basketball heartbreak. Zoë did the mother, opening every sentence with a dramatic "My child . . ." and I kept giving them more and more lines from the movie—I'm the one with the good memory. That night, before we fell asleep, Ron hugged his pillow and said, I think we should do this every week. I said: Great idea, and: Saturdays could work, they never give me this shift at the restaurant anyway. Zoë nodded a lot and looked stern.

Now Zoë says, Well, we haven't done anything about it, so I sort of thought it was off. Ron is disappointed; he stares at nothing without blinking. He doesn't want to pick a fight, though; he never does. Then he strokes my hair absentmindedly. Ron and I hardly ever have sex without Zoë anymore, and something in the way he strokes my hair explains why. Looks like it's just the two of us then, he tells me, but he's looking at Zoë.

After I slept with Ron the first time, on the floor of my old apartment in Hell's Kitchen (not because it was sexy but because the mattress was too small and smelled of the people who used to own it), we talked about Identity. Ron's family immigrated to the United States when he was in high school, after his father, an importer/exporter, couldn't make good on a deal he'd made with the Israeli Air Force. Ron said, I've always felt Israeli in America, but if I went back today I'm sure I'd be the American in Israel. You never know, I said, maybe you should try. I can't, he said, because of my dad. I didn't know how to answer that, so I didn't. Then he said, There's something I need to tell you. It's generally not what you want to hear when you can still feel the cold floor against your naked back, but I didn't mind it too much; his tone suggested potential, not threat. He said, I have a girlfriend, but it's not like that, we have an open relationship. I said, There's something I need to tell you, too: I've been mostly into women for the longest time; you're the first man I've been with in maybe five years. Really? I would never have thought that, he said. He stretched back until his head touched the book stand behind him; he looked at me like he was seeing something new, like he was disappointed in himself for having missed it before. I think you and Zoë might really like each other, he said; we should all go out sometime.

In my fantasy, our love is a visible thing. We don't even have to be together for people to see it. When I'm with Zoë, when I'm with Ron, when the two of them are without me, maybe even when one of us is walking down some street alone, people can tell that what they are seeing is part of something else, that a piece is missing. And when the three of us are together, people get it; they smile at us and suddenly they think, *Why not?*

Maybe there's something about our love they find inspiring. Maybe they look at us and forget what it is they are supposed to find strange. And maybe they, too, have more than one person they love, more than one person they call to trash Deli Guy who gave the wrong change again, more than one person whose morning breath they love waking up to.

But reality is often quite different. At a bar two blocks from the bookstore, Ron and I sit on barstools, looking something like a brother and sister who've just learned of a death in the family. I look at Ron's beer and realize it will take some time for him to get happy at this rate. I push my White Russian in his direction, but I know he'll say it's too sweet. He makes a face. I don't know how you drink this shit, he says. He's cranky, and I want to say something that would change that, but I'm thinking: Stalking, problem, greedy; my words are all wrong. It's not a friend, is it, he says, and there's no question mark at the end of his words. I shake my head. I mean, we know all her friends, he says, if it was really a friend she'd say his name. I wait a few seconds before I say in Hebrew, Ron, we don't know all of her friends.

Hebrew feels weird, like some secret code; Ron and I got used to speaking English between us because of Zoë, and gradually Hebrew started to feel like an intimate space we shouldn't be sharing. Occasionally a word would slip, but mostly we honor this unspoken agreement. I miss Hebrew sometimes; other times I try to imagine how the words might sound if I didn't understand their meaning, and I wish that I could listen to them from the outside and choose whether or not to get back in.

Ron learned at an early age how you can hide behind a new language, how you can wear a new identity so tight on your skin that you forget it's only a costume. This is what he taught me: (1) To conquer a language that's not your native tongue, you need to prioritize reading over sleeping. (2) Fighting your accent is not a good idea. Let it slide off when it feels ready, and until then embrace it, tell yourself it's cute. (3) When you're in a relationship, and two people share an understanding that the third one doesn't, language is a tricky business.

At the bar on Prince Street, I see Ron's hesitation as clearly as I see his eyes. He's too tired to fight it, he answers in Hebrew. *Az ma, ani stam idyot?* he asks. I touch the soft spot on the back of his hand, just below his wristwatch. You're not an idiot, I say, *Ata lo idyot*; you just need to believe in certain things to keep going, you know?

We drink quietly after that, my fingers still stroking his

hand. I had a whole thing planned for tonight, he says suddenly, and we're back to English; I wanted to go to the Ferris wheel on Coney Island. Can you do that at night? I ask, and Ron's voice is shaky when he says, I don't know, I haven't checked. Or we could go hang out in Central Park, I say—it's become a joke between the three of us because we've been meaning to do it for so long. Ron smiles, and I close my eyes and open my mouth to say, I think Zoë's been stalking Keith Buckley, but the words sting the bottom of my throat and stay there. I'm not sure what scares me more—that I'll say it and everything will change, that I'll say it and nothing will. So I just keep stroking Ron's hand, drawing small flowers and triangles with my finger.

When we walk home from the bar, the air is no longer crisp, and I try to think of the right word but I can't find it. All the words are in Hebrew now, and none of them describe the air accurately. Ron hands a dollar bill to every person on the street who asks for money, and also to a few who don't, because he believes in karma. I haven't been to a peace rally in five months, he says, it's the least I can do. I want to say that I don't see the connection, but I know it will only upset him. How do you have so many singles? I ask. I broke a twenty when you went to the bathroom, Ron says, but his mind is somewhere else. I see a guy across the street from us, and for a second I think it's Dreadlocks from the bookstore, but he disappears before I can be sure.

The apartment is all lit, and I realize Zoë and I forgot to

turn off the lights, but Ron shouts, Zo? Zoë?—and then one more time, Zoë. Now he's doubly pissed off—that Zoë's not here, that he let himself hope she was. He says, Jesus fucking Christ, are you girls physically incapable of turning the light off? Is it really so hard to remember? Or is it that you just don't give a flying fuck that we're throwing our money at Con Edison like they are some fucking charity organization? I say, Don't take it out on me, Ron, it's not fair. He says, You left the house together, didn't you? I say, I'm not talking about the lights. Ron takes a deep breath, and for a second he looks taller and more buff than he is. I'm sorry, he says.

I go to the kitchen and put water in the pot. Ron, do you want some tea? I shout, because I think he's in the bedroom. I'm right here, you don't need to shout, he says, standing by the island that separates the kitchen from the living room.

At two a.m., we are sleepy in front of the television, fighting our eyes, two parents whose daughter is out clubbing on a school night. I say what we've both been thinking for some time: Ron, she might not be coming home tonight. Do you think we should call her? he asks. Her cell phone is in the bedroom, I say. Zoë often forgets to take her cell phone; when she remembers, it's because I put it in her bag myself. Ron snorts and says, Of course. Well, do you want to go to sleep, then? he asks me. I guess we should, I say, but we keep sitting there for a few more minutes while Will and Grace are going to see a therapist together. Then Ron asks, Did she take her keys? And I say, I'm pretty sure she did. A few minutes later, I'm brushing my teeth and Ron is turning off all the lights.

The apartment is too quiet, our huge king-sized bed feels empty, and this is the word I think about: *Ra'av.* It means hunger, which is not what I'm feeling, and yet for a while it's the only word I have. *Ra'av* is not something that makes falling asleep easy. Ron hugs me and then grabs my ass, a butt cheek in each hand. He's hard now, and his thumb finds its favorite spot and starts to rub it, my thong a small sailboat with the help of his hand. Tiny waves are sending the promise of pleasure in a code my body reads well, but it feels wrong without Zoë; we have "rules," and according to them if one of us is absent or uninterested the other two can always go ahead, but what happens in love is that reality will begin to set its own rules.

I stop him, and his entire body stiffens instantly. Then he says, We'll have to figure something out, you know, if she's not coming back. His voice is cold, distant. Of course she's coming back, I say, and then I add, At some point. I always knew this would happen, Ron says, and I feel like he's talking to somebody else, somebody I can't see. Always, he says again, even before we met you. In a way, that's why, you know, he says, and now he looks me straight in the eyes, and it reminds me of the look he had that day on the floor, after our first time. That's why what? I ask, though I know the answer. I thought maybe this way, with you, we could give this thing a fair shot, he says, and then adds, You know, "monogamy." I've never seen him looking so lost. She was more into women back then, he says. I run my finger up and down the bridge of his nose. I want him to look at me but he won't, and for a second I think maybe I should go sleep in the living room, though I know it's a childish thought. If he cries, I think, then I'll hug him, and maybe a different conversation will start. But Ron doesn't cry. He is a lost man with no tears. I turn away.

I'm almost asleep when I hear Ron whispering something, and at first I think I'm already dreaming. What? I whisper back, and he sighs and waits, but then whispers again. I don't know how to be that guy, he says, I don't know how to be the guy who's okay with this. I think: Maybe you're not, and I'm afraid to say it, but eventually I do. Maybe you're not. I want to be, Ron says, and he sounds like he needs to clear his throat; I want to be the guy who makes both of you happy. I want to be the guy who helps you open your own restaurant, and I want to be the guy who looks at Zoë and sees only what's important, who doesn't care about the rest.

Ron, I say, I don't want to open my own restaurant.

This is my metaphor for how people in Israel treat suicide bombings and bombings in general: the flu. Some bombings are like a mild flu that doesn't even make you skip work. These are the bombings in a city other than your own, not too many casualties, nobody you know. Others are worse, the kind of flu that makes you vow you will from now on be grateful for your health every hour of every day. When the location is a café you used to frequent, or when some girl who went to school with you and moved up north in third grade loses an arm, it feels *real*. For a short while, death feels close.

Still, this is what you do: you call a friend who used to go to that café, a friend who knows that girl. You spend a few minutes talking about how horrible it is, how your idea of normal life is actually insane. You sigh, and your friend sighs as well, but at the end of that sigh there's already a new thought. Then you say the word "so" like that: So . . . And you ask your friend about the guy she was supposed to go out with last night. Your friend jumps at the opportunity like you knew she would; the guy she went out with last night was a weirdo who wouldn't stop talking about owls, but she fucked him anyway. Then, for thirty, thirty-five minutes, this is what you do: analyze. You analyze your friend's taste for men with odd obsessions, or you analyze your own need to occasionally stare at the sun until you cry, or you analyze a mutual friend's secret affair with a married man who once was your teacher.

You analyze, and slowly you notice how words like "tragedy" and "death" hold nothing more than their own sound. Tragedy, in that sense, becomes something like "chocolate" or "bicycle."

When I wake up, Ron and I are on different sides of the bed, facing up, and Zoë is lying on top of us, facedown and arms stretched to her sides, like some kind of collapsed Jesus. I stay still and breathe deeply. I feel happy, though I want to feel other things. This is what I'm thinking: Central Park.

I gently raise Zoë's arm and fold myself out of bed underneath it, then gently put her arm back on the mattress. I'm thinking: breakfast in bed. I'm thinking: something fancy. Ron and Zoë are always trying to get me to cook for them, and I always refuse, because who wants to bring their work home? But now I feel not only the wish but the *need* to cook; I want to chop, stir-fry, bake. I'm walking quietly out of the room, so as not to wake them, and I'm trying to remember what vegetables we have, whether or not we're out of eggs. I'm almost touching the bedroom door when something registers with me, something I must have seen right when I opened my eyes, but chose not to. I turn around, though I already know the answer: Ron, on top of the sheet that's supposed to be covering him, is wearing his blue Superman underwear. Last night, when I fell asleep, he was in his gray plaid boxers.

In an instant, I feel sick. The thought of the two of them having sex without me—no, next to me—and choosing not to wake me up, makes me feel as if I already made breakfast for three people and then ate it by myself. I run to the bathroom; I want to throw up all the pastries, the omelet, the coffee I never had. I make gagging sounds, and I no longer care about waking them up; I sound like an animal. But nothing comes out, and as far as I can tell, Ron and Zoë are still sound asleep.

Then there are two *Me*s.

Me No. 1 is the Israeli who was taught that being tough and being strong are the same thing. She was a soldier once, for two long years, so she believes she can survive anything. She says: You're chasing after something that doesn't exist. She says: You'll be just fine on your own. This is what she believes I should do: pack my stuff. She's thinking about the blue suitcase, about taking it out of the bedroom closet without knocking down Ron's old speakers. She's thinking about how much she could fit in the suitcase, how many back-and-forths it would take. She's thinking about where she could go.

Me No. 2 is a woman who successfully impersonates an American. She is soft-spoken, and once a week she gets lost in the city on purpose, then walks—no maps, no questions—until she finds her way home. She has a lot to prove. She says: This isn't the end.

Sometimes, when the three of us are together, my body feels like marshmallow, calm and weightless. That Saturday three weeks ago is a good example, and I see it now: we are rolling off our cushions in laughter, holding our stomachs like footballs. I think, Who is this person? That me who isn't Israeli and isn't American, isn't gay and isn't straight—who is she?

For a while I just listen to the Sunday-morning quiet, interrupted every few seconds by Ron's snoring. But all of a sudden I think: What if this isn't the first time? I feel Ron hugging me from behind in the bathroom one morning, and

I hear his voice: You're totally dead to the world when you're asleep, you know that? I start gagging again, and I can't stop.

Zoë's voice comes to me through the gagging sound, through the bathroom door: You okay, babe? Can I come in? I throw up now, finally, but I'm vomiting water and air, and I feel like I'm suffocating. I hold the door with my left hand to keep Zoë from coming in, because our bathroom doesn't have a lock. As a result, I have to let go of my hair, and when I throw up again it gets splashed.

When I get up to brush my teeth, Zoë opens the door. I'm fine, I say before she has a chance to ask. Are you sick or something? she asks. I'm fine, I say again, tasting toothpaste. I'm sorry about yesterday, she says, it wasn't cool of me to leave you and go with that guy. She clings to my back now, hugs my shoulders, and looks at both of us in the bathroom mirror. Besides, he kind of smelled like burnt rubber, she says in an attempt to make me smile. I don't. You know it's not you, Pie, she whispers in my ear, and then kisses it; it's just my fucking daddy issues, it has nothing to do with you. But I'll work on it, she adds when I don't respond, I will. I try to ignore her and focus on brushing my teeth; she reaches for my toothbrush with her right hand, and I stop brushing and look in the mirror. We look stupid; I have white toothpaste foam coming out of my mouth, and Zoë's eyes are still sticky with sleep. I look sad; she looks relaxed. She kisses my cheek, her eyes still on the mirror. Ron and I had a really good talk when I got home, she says softly; everything will be okay, you'll see. Her voice is all promise, and I feel a sharp pain at the bottom of my stomach, my need to believe her.

I spit and say slowly, What about Keith Buckley? Zoë's eyes go from the mirror to the sink. She says, I don't want to talk about it; and then, It's not important. I say, Maybe it is. Zoë lets her head fall gently to one side, and her fingers circle the zipper of her sweatshirt. When they settle on it, they pull it down a bit, then up, again and again. She says, I just . . . I got it in my head that if Keith doesn't notice me, then it's a sign that I'll never succeed in anything, you know? She looks at me now. But I'm done, Pie, I swear, she says and shakes her head. Done. I put my hand over hers, quieting her zipper. Zo, it's impossible not to notice you, I say. Zoë gives a short laugh, and we stand there like that for a few seconds. Then she says, Remember that guy with the dreadlocks from the bookstore? The weirdest thing happened. I saw him again when I was on my way back, and he just walked up to me, in the middle of the street at like four a.m., and said, Go home. Maybe it wasn't him, I say, maybe it was some crazy guy. It was him, Zoë says, I recognized him, and I'm sure he recognized me, too. What did you do? I ask her. I don't know, she says, it was this moment from a dream; I think I said, That's what I'm doing, I'm going home.

Almost out the door, she turns around and says, But listen, Pie, the Keith stuff, that's just between us, okay? I wait, then ask, Why? She's already on her way to the kitchen, her arm stretching in front of her to open the freezer door. She giggles and says, You're the best, Pie, because she thinks my question is a clever way of saying "of course." This is what I think: Nothing's changed.

I am alone in the bathroom now. I look at myself in the mirror, foam-free. I hear Zoë in the kitchen fixing us all a Saturday-morning breakfast. I'm no longer nauseated, and the idea of breakfast is tempting. The only thing Zoë knows how to make is French toast, but it's the best I've ever tasted. I think: This is what there is, this is my life. I think: Do I want it or not?

Zoë turns on the stereo to wake Ron up. Radiohead or Coldplay? she shouts, but doesn't wait for an answer. Then she's in the bathroom again, holding a bottle of maple syrup. I think she's about to ask what's taking me so long, but this is what she says: Ron thinks I should go to Israel with you in the summer; he says we'd have a blast and that we shouldn't miss out just because of him. What do you say?

I see us on the plane, right before landing, and I hear people clapping as the wheels hit the ground. Zoë laughs. I've told her about this silly Israeli tradition, the way I've told her so many other Israel stories, the way I've been telling her about Tel Aviv since the day we met. I say, It's stupid, you know; this culture treats pilots as heroes. Zoë says, It's not stupid, and then: It's exciting. She tugs on my earlobe the way she sometimes does, and peeks out the tiny airplane window. Then she says, We need to call Ron right when we land; we promised. I say, We will, but I don't think he's worried.

Ron ducks under Zoë's arm to get into the bathroom. He starts to pee, but then his face twitches. It smells like puke in here, he says. Then he looks at me, still peeing. You all right?

VICTOR, CHANGED MAN

I. Natalie's Return

Two a.m. on a dreary Tuesday, a knock on the door and Natalie was in the doorway, her eyes shining more purple than ever. I immediately went to the bedroom and shook Stuart and Martha awake. This was lovely, I said when Stuart opened his eyes, looking at me like he couldn't quite place me, but I need you and your wife to leave now; the woman I love is suddenly in the doorway, against all odds.

The man Natalie left was a very different version of me. Two years later, I am no longer him. He was a reckless mess: the kind of man who looks up at the moon on a gray night and starts laughing; the kind of man who treats ointments as gifts. Beauty, then, was a code I was trying to break.

She just woke up one morning, looked at me, and

started packing. I couldn't blame her. She was out before the first bird started singing, which I've always been grateful for. Asleep, I was spared the humiliation of pleading.

I've always assumed she was done with me for good, in part because the note she left said, "Victor, I'm done with you for good."

2. The Fog of the Morning After

In my living room, Natalie showed no interest in conversation. She let her hands look for answers in my pants, or else she had no questions at all. I said, Nat, you will be happy to hear that I am now a changed man, a better man. I said, I think we should discuss the terms on which . . . But Natalie's left hand made me forget what I wanted to discuss.

The last thing I remember that night is Natalie saying, No way, Victor, I've got to get some sleep, when I grazed the space between her breasts with my thumb for the third time. I didn't mean . . . I said; I just wanted to feel close to you. That was a lie—I did mean. I meant to have sex with Natalie again because her skin was smooth like Teflon, and every time I thought maybe now I'll get a good grip. But Natalie must have believed me, because she said, You've always confused sex with comfort, Victor. That's your problem.

Already, I had a problem again.

This was five a.m., and within seconds Natalie was grinding her teeth next to me, and I thought, God, I missed her. I do remember looking out the window and thinking, This is one foggy night, but it didn't seem like anything the morning would fail to disperse. My last thought before closing my eyes was this: If Natalie doesn't notice my change, or if she leaves before she does, have I actually changed at all?

By the time Natalie and I woke up, the cloud consistency must have been at stage two if not three, and you could see nothing except your own thoughts. Natalie? I said, and my question mark hung heavy in the foggy air, suggesting for a moment that last night was just another fantasy. Natalie said, Victor, I'm scared. I followed the sound of her voice, hands stretched forward until I felt her body, and she said, Ouch, because apparently I got her straight in the eye. Jesus, Victor, Jesus Christ, she kept saying, and we started to walk carefully toward the bathroom so she could wash her eye. Did you put something on your fingernails, Victor? Natalie asked; it burns like hell. In my tiny bathroom we found better prospects. The square metal-framed window looked like a floating silver cube, emanating light. What is that? Natalie asked, sounding pissed instead of happy. I said, Light, light, we can see light through that window! This is east, I added, we're turning east now, so I guess maybe things are not as bad in the east. That doesn't make *any* sense, Victor, Natalie said and sighed.

I almost said: Nat, this isn't my fault, or: At least we can see each other now, or: Nat, try to cheer up. But I thought:

Change change change. So I sat down next to her on the edge of the bathtub, touched her chin gently, and said, Nat, It's going to be okay, I promise.

3. Faux Heroism

The fog took almost three days to clear. By the end of the second day, fog clearers were threatening to go on strike, and Natalie said, I knew it, I knew it. She meant that government people always look for excuses not to work. Or she meant she should never have come back to me; Natalie hates government people, but she also often regrets her choices, so it was hard to tell.

I said, Nat, maybe we can clear some fog on our own. She said, That's stupid, there's only two of us. I said, We can form a posse, recruit people with good intentions. This was my only chance to prove to Natalie how changed I was. Suddenly I felt an appetite for leadership. I drew road maps, diversion plans, tools we might need. But then I looked at Natalie. She was shaking her head. It's not our job, Victor, she said; the government's supposed to do it. I should have known, of course, that's what Natalie would say. She used to have a Don't Enable Incompetence sticker. She believed passivity was the purest form of protest. What kind of changed man was I, to forget my girlfriend's values? It was too late, and I figured honesty was all I had left. I said, I'm trying to show you growth here, Natalie, just give me a chance. That's not growth, Natalie said; that's faux heroism, very common among males in your age group.

By that time we could see each other clearly, and every hour the world outside looked a little more like something you could trust. The satellite signal kept coming and going, and Natalie spent her hours staring at the screen so as not to miss the next time when the clouds and the winds and the satellite plates all aligned themselves in a way that allowed news reporters to appear briefly in my living room, explaining things about cloud consistency and evacuation efforts, providing updates about the cleaners' strike. To Natalie, these were things of great importance. A woman needs a good countdown when she wants to leave a man.

I wasn't exactly sure what faux heroism meant, but with our reunion at a state of such acute fragility, I couldn't afford any ignorance. I didn't ask. I thought, Maybe there's a thing called faux heroism that masquerades as change in grown men fighting for love; I thought, Maybe that's why I kept doubting my change, kept questioning its veracity; I thought, Maybe once again, Natalie is right.

On the morning of the fourth day, when we woke up, we could see the mountains through my bedroom window, and I knew we were down to minutes. Really, it was safe enough to leave the night before, but Natalie was being kind. She stretched and said, Morning, in her sleepy voice; already, I was missing her. I stared out the window, hating the mountains, the clear horizon. I said, Just no notes this time, okay?

She rolled herself on top of me, smelling of dreams, and said, No notes, I promise, and I knew I should make our last time long enough to hold a little bit of future, long enough to be both a moment and a memory.

4. Flowers Wilt in Sexless Air

It's been a week now since Natalie left, and I'm gravely considering abandoning this righteous version of me, going back to the old one. Change, I've learned, is rarely a good idea. If only I could stop imagining Natalie's purple eyes watching everything I do, there would be nothing left to consider, and I would be my old self again: immature, unreliable, self-centered. But those eyes, they're the toughest audience a man can have. For now, I keep trying.

One problem: when Natalie left again, she must have taken with her any physical desire I've ever had. For the first time in my life, my body is numb with indifference.

When Martha comes over to visit, she looks at my window box with concern and says, Even your flowers can't take it anymore. At first I assume she just wants my attention—I've felt that sort of thing from Martha a couple times before, back when she and Stuart were living with me—but then I look and see she's right: the flowers in my window box are wilting. I still can't do it. I feel inadequate, too selfish even for plants, too selfish to take care of anything more alive than a wall. My flowers are begging for the chemical sex releases to the air, and I can't give it to them. I think: Maybe I can at least have sex with myself? But I cringe at the thought; it feels like I just threw up and someone is offering me candy. I think: I never should have gotten that window box, I'm too self-absorbed for gardening; I think: Selfish is the opposite of changed. Then I think, Well, when I bought it, I never knew Natalie would come back, then leave again; I had every intention to produce enough chemicals for many, many flowers. But then I think: My poor flowers; they don't care about reasons, they just want to live.

While I am thinking all these thoughts, Martha is tidying up my room, folding clothes, spraying Lysol. It stinks of loneliness in here, she says and pouts, her nose a small wrinkled button.

I look at Martha and say, If you and Stuart are willing to go at it for my flowers, you can live here rent-free. She says, We don't pay bills and we don't pay for food. Deal, I say.

5. Charisma and the Average Woman

Three a.m. on a bleak Monday night, and Stuart is suddenly in my bedroom. She's not coming back, he says. Jesus, I know that, what the fuck, I say. I meant Martha, he says. Martha's gone? I say; we had a deal—what about my flowers? Then I feel bad for asking that first. I'm sorry, man, I say. But I'm not really; I can't feel too much these days.

Then I feel bad for not genuinely feeling bad, and I know the night is over. I sit up in my bed. So what happened? I ask Stuart and realize: I am a changed man, a man who cares enough to ask questions; I cannot be unchanged.

Stuart says, You know how women are about charisma. I say, I'm not sure. He says, You know, the whole concept of audience—they need it, like, constantly. They do? I ask. Oh sure, he says. It's all projections and shit, you know. If you're not a good audience, they don't feel charismatic. If they don't feel charismatic, they're not in the mood to fuck. Then there's no sex, your flowers start to die, and you're fantasizing about other men, and then they catch you and say, So the whole threesome business, the whole orgy business—all this time you were simply gay. Every time it's the same bullshit, man, and I'm sick of it.

Charisma, huh, I say. Charisma, he says, and fingers my cheekbones.

6. A Call for Action

In the kale aisle a week later, Stuart and I are choosing our greens when Martha appears. Look, I don't care what you two got going on, she says, that's not why I'm here. How many times do I have to tell you, Stuart says. Martha rolls her eyes. I thought you might want to know, she says, looking at me: the fog's not gone; they just pushed it over to the docks. It's always something about the docks with you, Stuart says; not *everyone* is out to get the poor *all the time*, Martha. She ignores him. Natalie is stuck there, she tells me. I just thought you should know.

As I am throwing things into my large backpack, Stuart says, It's probably not even true. I can't take that chance, I tell him. We'd have heard about it, he says, if things down there really got *so* bad. I give him a look. You know very well if the government doesn't want something reported, it doesn't get reported, I say. Either way, he says, she's not your problem anymore; isn't that the point of breaking up? I tell him I won't let anything bad happen to her. Stop it, Stuart says, you know the hero talk turns me on; why would you do that when you're practically out the door?

7. A Whole Lot of Something Else

Closest I can drop you off are the downtown gates, the cabdriver says, no cars going to the docks anymore. I nod at him through the rearview mirror. I don't understand how no one is talking about this, I say. He shrugs. It ain't news when there ain't nothing new about it, he says. It's fogged like this before? I ask, but of course he's not talking about the fog; he's talking about the government moving problems instead of solving them. He looks at me to see if I'm being funny. Ain't no fog in the Main City now, is there, he says.

When he stops the car, I can't see the gates; everything ahead of us is a gray shade of white. I am still, my fingers not reaching for money. In my own apartment I couldn't find Natalie without hurting her eye; why did I think I could save her? I imagine walking into something sharp, and dying, the blood pouring out of me invisible in the fog. No harm in changing your mind, my man, the cabdriver says; this wouldn't be my first round trip today. You don't understand, I say, still not moving. Sure I do, he says, you got a woman in there. He turns around and looks at me, squints to see better. Or maybe a man? he asks, and then concludes, Someone you love. I do, I say, but that's hardly the point. The cabdriver chuckles—perhaps thinking I'm joking, perhaps laughing at me. For years I was a man who'd never give a massage unless he wanted one himself, I tell him, who'd never make a salad for someone unless he himself was hungry. But I'm trying to change, I say, my voice cracking on the last word. Then go home and make a salad for someone, the cabdriver says; hell, bake them a pie! This here is a whole lot of something else. Just give me a minute, I ask. It's your dime, my man, he says, but let me tell you. I seen ready and I seen unready, and you sure ain't in the first group.

The wheels make an awful sound when we're U-turning, and I wonder if it's the engine or some animal trapped underneath it.

8. A Full Garden

Every time the doorbell rings, I imagine Natalie ringing it. Victor, she says, I've heard rumors that you've truly changed; are they true? Nat, I say, shaking, you're alive. I was never in the docks, Natalie says, or she says, Yes, I got away. She looks behind me then, and her eyes widen. Victor, it's like a full garden in here. It's not what you think, Nat, I tell her; I haven't been with anyone in a long time. I believe you, Natalie says, and I believe you've truly changed. I nod, tears in my eyes. Sometimes at that point she says, Victor, I'd like you to meet your son, and behind her I see a child, a beautiful boy with my skin and purple eyes. I pull both of them close to me and we hug. Come in, I tell them, come in.

WAIT

Wait with the babies, would you? By which I mean, make sure she's on the pill. We have been divorced for a while now, but we were married for many years; that means I have no right to ask you to wait, but you have no right to refuse me.

You don't know who I'm talking about, but she will be blond. A year from now, you'll be having an argument in a restaurant uptown. It will be about green olives—you keep forgetting she's allergic—but it will be about fear. Her fear of losing you, her fear of me.

It's possible that her blond hair is making her prone to excessive insecurity. You might want to look into that.

Except, honey, she'll be right. It's a scary thing, dating someone with a past like ours. You still had decades of marriage left in you when I asked you to cook only when you're hungry.

I never meant to leave you, you know. I just woke up one morning having left you, and so I left you again, because what's the sense in arguing with reality?

So, honey, run after her, would you? I know how you feel about running, I know all about your bad knee. Just listen. Forget about the check, silly. You can always go back the next day. And look around you—would they go out of business over two unpaid filets? So run. You never knew when to grab and when to let go, I've always had to tell you. And so I'm telling you now.

When you catch up to her—she'll run like a woman who wants your hand to grab her shoulder from behind, which is to say slowly—lie. Express feelings you don't yet feel, make promises you're not sure you can keep. You are a truthful man, I know. But darling, in love, a lie makes a clearing for truth to come in.

I know you must find this confusing. I am confusing you. That was the problem, wasn't it? I always confused you and you kept trying to follow me. I led us down some spiral roads, and when we reached the bottom we saw reflections of us looking frustrated and old. I would say, Please take responsibility for these people we don't know; it hurts my eyes to look at them. And you'd say, I take full responsibility and I apologize and can I get you some eyedrops? You always wanted to get me eyedrops.

It may not appear this way, but what I'm doing is trying to climb back up that spiral road. Some days my muscles hurt but I keep going because I'm reading books that tell me to lean in to the pain. I lean in to my pain until I twitch, until I shake. Unfortunately, twitching and shaking are not things one can lean in to—I've tried. The outcome involves falling.

Your silence is asking me what I truly want—which is to say I am asking myself. That was my earlier point about reflections, but that's not important now.

I want you to run after her. When you grab her shoulder from behind, I want you to pretend to be out of breath. It's not hard, for God's sake—just fake short, quick breaths and pull her close to your chest. I want you to promise her you'll never forget about her olive allergy again. I want you to tell her your forgetfulness is not a sign of anything, and certainly has nothing to do with me. I want you to make up some bullshit story that explains your behavior. You know how your parents never remember what foods you dislike? You can work with that. She'll believe anything, because she'll want to. And I want you to make her believe. Hold her tight for a few minutes. It'll be cold and windy, but darling, you really need to man up about winter. When she stops crying,

I want you to kiss her. I want you to look into her eyes and say something horribly cliché like The past is in the past. My sense is she will not be the type sensitive to clichés. But say it like you mean it, honey, because what I'm telling you is that eventually you will. And throw my name in there when you say it. She needs to see that you can say my name without pain in your chest. Don't let her see the pain in your chest.

But darling, wait. We held each other's hands in hospital rooms, we laughed for three days once, we spoke complete sentences in unison. We loved through our twenties, and we turned thirty together, four years apart. And one warm September we invited two hundred and seventy people and promised all of them that we would love each other forever, and in return these people gave us money, and gifts.

So when she cooks that special meal and buys that sexy nightgown—I've mentioned she's not bothered by clichés—and tells you she wants to have your baby, wait. Would you wait? Remember the song you recorded for me. Remember that drive up north on my birthday. Remember our first date, your grandmother's old Beetle. So many hours we spent in cars, singing. Just wait.

Tell her now isn't a good time. Tell her you don't have enough money saved up yet. And tell her you'll probably get there eventually—set a date to discuss babies again. Say, Let me get through this next round of fund-raising and then I'll know more. Compliment her on the steak—because isn't it nice to be with a meat eater, and isn't it nice to be with someone who cooks—but stop eating when she shows you the nightgown. Pretend to have lost all interest in the food. I know you never lose interest in food, honey, but what I'm saying is sometimes it's okay to pretend. So pretend. You'll have a great night, you'll see.

But call me the next day. Would you call me? Tell me she wants to start trying and I'll say, Trying what. I can be thick when I want to avoid pain. Be gentle with me. Explain. I'll ask what *you* want, how you feel. I'll pretend that this is a conversation we can have. But at the end, right before we hang up, I'll hold my breath and whisper, Wait. Would you hear me? Would you wait?

DOCUMENTATION

Kisses #1–3

I kiss you for the first time, and it starts to rain. You tell me it's a sign of something, maybe good luck. We don't have an umbrella, so we just stand there kissing, getting wet, and I think about what you said. The idea that the sky is talking to us makes me uncomfortable, but I don't say that, and hug you instead. You mistake my hug for agreement, and let your face sink into my shoulder. The air smells clean.

The second time I kiss you is an attempt to comfort; you've just found out your cat died. I don't like cats, but that would clearly be the wrong thing to say, so I think maybe a kiss could fill in for words. Your sadness makes your lips soft, too soft, and I feel like I'm shaping a kiss out of Play-Doh. You know the difference between passion and empathy, of course; you stop me, your left hand between our mouths. I walk away from you; this is noon and New York and the street is roaring. You are alone now with your distance, with your sorrow, with the memory of your dead cat.

I kiss you a third time, two weeks later, and it's a good kiss—just the right balance of wetness and dryness, closeness and a sense of self. You are the reason this kiss is a success, this is your accomplishment. I am impressed, and decide to document every lip encounter between us from now until there is nothing more to document. This will be three years later, in an ice-cream parlor on Sixth Avenue, where you will kiss me with chocolate-chip cookie dough and finality, and I will let my ice cream drip all over my new tank top after you've gone, like in a bad movie.

For now, documenting helps me forget what I don't yet know.

Kiss #17

I kiss you in a swimming pool. The lightness of my body in the water makes me feel inconsequential. I try to leave my frustration out of our kiss, but that's the thing about kisses, isn't it? You can never leave anything out.

The smell of chlorine stays in my skin for two days. I take multiple showers, because I don't know how to passively wait for things to get better. You say that I'm crazy, that I'm imagining things, imagining the chlorine. I pretend the smell is gone before it really is.

Kiss #99

This is a Sunday-morning kiss in upstate New York. We are at a bed-and-breakfast. It has been a long time since you kissed me like this, and it reminds me of that kiss that made me fall in love with you (see kiss #3). Yesterday was filled with disappointment; we got lost and couldn't find I-87, then the hot tub wasn't as big as you'd expected. But this kiss, the first thing that happens to me on Sunday, is light with possibility and future.

Kiss #146

This is the kiss that tells me the rules have changed. I clearly taste salami, which I know you don't eat, and your tongue is doing something it's never done before: some kind of loop to the left, then to the right; it feels calculated and foreign, and my mouth goes numb.

Kiss #147

I kiss you again, two hours later—an attempt to replace the memory. You would never let me kiss you if you knew my motivation, because you think I'm always treating life as if it's a film and pretending to be the director. I want this kiss (#147) to prove the former (#146) wrong. It does not. I decide to ignore it, ignore the salami.

Kiss #163

The promise kiss. *There's something I need to tell you*, you say, and Salami has a name now, though I refuse to repeat it. You promise me that it's all behind us. You say it was just a slip, and I keep thinking, Slip, slip, slip of the lip.

Kiss #212

This kiss tells me you're bored again. We are at MoMA (this is before they closed, before they renovated, before they reopened; by then we will not be together). We look at a beautiful black woman Chris Ofili made from elephant dung. The couple next to us finds it romantic. They laugh, and mid-laughter the man grabs the woman by her shoulders. It's a powerful gesture; his hands are telling her he is sure.

We look at them, and it seems that we're supposed to

follow. But in our kiss there is nothing but habit. I realize then that we are not really done with Salami—that when you let things like that in, they can never find the way out.

Kiss #288

Kiss #288 gives me false hope, which, without the perspective of time, appears simply as hope.

We are visiting your parents in California, and it is going well. I've already met your dad when he was in New York on business, but everyone knows it is the mother who decides how the parents feel. She will announce her verdict with her arms, I know, when she hugs you goodbye before we leave. But this will only happen in two days, and now, on the evening of our arrival, everyone is tired except us, though we are the ones who should be sleepy, with our internal clocks still on East Coast time. You sneak into the bathroom when I go there to pee, and we kiss with the excitement of teenage rebels.

Kisses #289–301

These kisses are an attempt to relive that bathroom kiss, kiss #288. We look for dark places, inappropriate places, places lived in by people we don't even know. When there are no more excuses for hiding, we hide in private and pretend it's the same. When we can no longer pretend, we lie. Hiding was something we found exciting for a while, we say, and now we're over it. When the lie is exposed, we look the other way. I know what you are thinking: we're like the worst poker players on earth, refusing to look at the cards we are holding.

When winter comes, I know the end is close. When I tremble at night because the window is cracked, you hold me, and you let your hands run up and down my back, my arms; but there are no more kisses. All winter long I wait for you to show up with empty boxes, a duffel bag, something that can host your belongings as they depart from shelves and drawers. I say nothing about it, and clean the apartment twice every day because I don't know how to passively wait for things to get worse. When I cry one evening for no reason, you kiss my tears, and I wonder whether or not it counts, whether or not it should be documented. By the end of winter I know, the way events sometimes unfold in a woman's mind before their time, that our first ice cream this summer will be our last.

THE DISNEYLAND OF ALBANY

Avner had woken up too late. Only when he walked over to get the coffee going, his electric toothbrush humming along—how Netta used to hate that—and caught a glimpse of the clock on the kitchen counter did he realize he'd miscalculated. How had that happened? He'd set two different alarms to two-fifteen a.m., was half awake the whole night, but by two-fifteen, he now realized, he should have already been on his way. He felt terror at the thought of his little girl waiting for him alone at JFK in the middle of the night. She wouldn't be alone, would she? There would be a flight attendant taking care of her, there always was, but he'd never been late, and so who knew how that worked. He started moving fast, throwing last things into his suitcase, bumping into everything in his speed. What a bad idea it all was, this trip to Albany.

From a distance it looked like they were laughing, Maya and this stranger in uniform, but perhaps he was wrong, because by the time he got closer they both seemed annoyed. Maymay, he said a bit too loud, and hugged his daughter. It always took her some time to warm up to him, and he could understand that, no reason to take it personally. Photo ID, please, the flight attendant said in Hebrew, looking at Maya but obviously meaning him. So sorry I'm late, Avner said, and handed her his passport. It was the normal procedure, and her rudeness was normal, too, for an Israeli, and yet he couldn't help but feel . . . criticized. Was this only about his lateness, or did Netta perhaps say something about him when she dropped Maya off? Sorry, Avner said again, although the woman had clearly heard him the first time; I'm really sorry.

Now it was five a.m., and Avner and Maya were making their way through the Penn Station crowd. Where were all these people rushing to so early in the morning? Avner was anxious that he would lose Maya. He tried again. Come on, why not give me your hand? But she'd said it earlier—his hand was sweaty. She made her cheek and shoulder meet, indicating her no-thank-you. Avner wished to find himself in a world where grown men could do that too, make their cheek and shoulder meet.

He could see she was looking at his beret. Or was she? He might be imagining it, which would be Netta's fault.

When Netta called to announce that "the package has been shipped," right before they hung up she said, Avner, one more thing. Don't wear that silly hat, okay? It embarrasses her. What an awful word, *embarrass.* This isn't Israel, Netta, he said; in New York, people wear whatever they want. People wear whatever they want in Tel Aviv, too, Netta replied, only here when you look ridiculous they tell you to your face. And then—she's a little girl, Avner, and she's getting to that age. Just don't wear the hat. Avner exhaled into the phone. Netta, he said slowly, if my daughter wants to ask me something, she can ask me herself. Occasionally, since moving to New York, he was able to stand up to Netta in these small ways. You're such a teenager, Avner, Netta said.

Maya was carrying a purple backpack, and he was carrying her TIME magazine duffel bag and his own suitcase. It was incredible, how long Netta managed to hang on to things like crappy duffel bags they'd gotten *for free* years ago. The weight of it made him twist as he walked, and he wanted to call Netta and ask if she was ever going to buy a trolley suitcase like a normal person. But he didn't, of course, and what was new about that? They'd always been experts at not saying things to each other.

Maya seemed to be looking at the drops of sweat trickling down his forehead. It was genetic, this sweating; his father had sweated just this way before him—fast, face-first. You've been spared, little girl, he wanted to say, be grateful. But suddenly she wasn't next to him. A split second of horror, as if he'd inhaled ice instead of air, and then he spotted her, three steps behind. Her pigtails were messed up from the plane, and she had stopped to undo them. His chest felt like it was a couple seconds ahead, already on its way to reach her. He quickly closed the gap between them. Need help with that? he asked. She raised her eyes as if seeing him for the first time, and pulled out the second hair tie, her face slightly twitching from the effort. She put both hair ties in her pocket, and he said, Maya, let me know when you need to stop, okay? I don't want to lose you. She nodded.

They kept walking, but where? The signs all looked the same. Numbers, arrows, words. Signs in this country always confused him, and transportation hubs of all kinds were enormous; in Israel he'd have easily found his way by now. He turned his head to his side every few seconds, trying to keep his daughter in sight. It occurred to him how trusting she was, never doubting that he was leading them to the right place. He wanted to be worthy of that trust, but he also had the urge to teach her never to trust anyone unless she knew what to do if that person fucked up. He wanted to teach her that people very often fucked up.

Looking ahead, he saw the information booth. He stopped, and she immediately stopped as well. That way, he said, pointing and trying to sound authoritative. Maya followed him, but suddenly seemed suspicious. Two people were in line, and Avner and Maya stood behind them. That's where the train's supposed to be? Maya asked. How quick, these shifts, how sharp. Up until just now, at least he was the dad who knew how to get to the train. We're very close, Avner said.

On the train, the Netta in his head was berating him for his bad judgment, the needlessness of this trip. Poor Maya, she was saying, being dragged like that after such a long flight. (In reality, when he told Netta about the plan for this visit she only said, Sounds nice, and he appreciated that.) An art collector calls, you go, he said to imaginary Netta now; that's just how it is for artists in New York. He would look her straight in the eyes, too; what did she know about his life in New York? She hardly asked him anything anymore. You could have pushed her visit back a few days, he heard Netta say. With few words, she was winning the argument; Netta was incapable of losing. Because, yes, wouldn't it have been better? Easier for Maya, easier for him. But he couldn't bring himself to do it. It would have meant a shorter visit, three days lost. And he was seeing so little of her, it seemed criminal.

Maya was sleeping in the seat next to him now, hugging her backpack, and her hands looked so small that for a moment he thought perhaps he should talk to Netta about it, perhaps Maya's hands weren't developing properly. He leaned over and whispered, We're going to have fun, Maymay. You'll see.

His cell phone vibrated in his pocket, and he knew it was Gillian before he looked. Maybe he should have said yes, let her come. He almost never met a collector without Gillian; she was the one finding these buyers for him, affluent Jewish people, for the most part, who loved art or wanted to love art, or who Gillian thought might confuse supporting Avner with supporting Israel. And she'd have known her way around once they got to Albany—she'd lived there at some point, if he wasn't mistaken—and maybe that would have allowed Avner to be less tense, more attentive to Maya. He assumed she understood, when he mentioned his daughter's visit, that he'd take this one alone, and was surprised when she still asked. *Should I tag along?* She wasn't even his gallerist, not yet—he needed to get more recognition for her to take him on—and while they worked together toward that, and while she was someone who seemed to believe in him as an artist, which meant a whole lot, wouldn't they be crossing some line if she were coming on this trip with him, meeting his *daughter*? And he could see it, that was the truth, as if watching a film: Maya in the kitchen back in Tel Aviv; Netta with her back to her, chopping a salad. This woman was also there with me and Daddy, she speaks Hebrew but kind of funny. And Netta says, Really? How nice—in a tone that doesn't give a thing away to the girl—but deep down she now thinks even less of him, if that's possible, and she starts chopping just a bit faster. Would Netta have confronted him then? *Are you seeing someone?* Probably not. It's been over two years now, and they've learned to—what, exactly?—not ask questions.

Ma kore, Gillian was asking, *atem al rakevet?* They spoke Hebrew sometimes—Gillian's Hebrew was surprisingly decent, considering she'd only lived in Israel a short time, years ago—and the truth was he found it sexy, her American accent rounding the rough edges, making the throaty sound of Hebrew softer, more accepting. He didn't want to feel that now, not with Maya there. Yup, on the train, he answered in English; what's up? We can talk later if it's a bad time, Gillian said. How different she was from Netta, how easily hurt. No, no, Avner said, I'm just quiet because Maya is sleeping, go ahead. I talked to Abe, Gillian said. Apparently, the art would be for a new office space he has up there—not for his home, like I thought—so keep that in mind. Avner wasn't sure how exactly to keep that information in mind. Gillian had a special talent—she knew who would buy and who wouldn't, who would like what. His brain didn't work that way, but he often felt he had to pretend. That's how artists were in New York, they knew how to play the game. Got it, he said. And, Gillian said and paused, he sounds very . . . pro-Israel, which is good for us. Right, Avner said.

So once again only his "Israeli work" would be considered, and again after the meeting Gillian would probably push him to produce more of it. Maybe he should simply give up on the rest, on his actual work—he was doing conceptual, surreal self-portraits these days, and it was going well—and accept that these silly drawings he made off of old stills of various places in Israel were the only thing that sold, the only thing people in New York liked. He wanted to ask if she'd gotten a better idea why this trip was necessary, why he and Abe couldn't meet in New York, but what difference did it make? He was already on his way, and it would only annoy her if he brought that up again. Gillian got impatient whenever he sounded unappreciative. I don't know, Avner, she would say; I thought you really needed the money right now. Money seemed to be the end of so many conversations in New York. He needed it, they had it. So anything they wanted him to do—say, travel to Albany with his daughter, probably for no other reason than to establish a power dynamic—he did. I'm pretty sure this trip will be worth your while, Gillian said now. That's exactly why she was successful—she easily intuited other people's concerns. I wasn't complaining, Avner said, though they both knew, of course, that wasn't exactly true. Oh, I'm sorry, Maymay, he said, though his daughter was still sleeping beside him, did I wake you up? Maya opened her eyes then, which startled him. She used to sleep through anything when she was little. She looked at him without speaking—Netta's daughter, no doubt—and Gillian said, Okay, you have to go, just one more thing, he particularly liked the Nuweiba series, so play that up. Sure thing, he said. Don't be like that, Avner, Gillian said. Be like what, he said, I'm saying I got it, no problem. Gillian sighed. Call me after the meeting if we don't talk before then, she said.

Maya's eyes were still on him when he got off the phone. What could he say that wouldn't be a lie? I didn't mean to wake you, he told her. Who were you talking to? she asked. He was probably imagining the judgment in her voice. In English he could say, A friend who's helping me sell paintings, a business acquaintance, but Hebrew doesn't ever allow you to avoid gender. And he had nothing to hide, did he? It's just work, he said, and Maya squinted, a small replica of Netta letting him know without words that she didn't believe him.

But was he lying? Often it seemed the only thing about him that interested Gillian was his Israeliness. Couldn't she see he wasn't that guy—the typical Israeli macho, the man who lived eleven months of every year waiting for his chance to leave his family and reunite with his army buddies and M16 on reserve duty, the man with a Middle Eastern temper and eyes that followed every skirt? When they first met—Gillian visited the studios at the residency he got, the residency that was his excuse for leaving Israel—he tried to bring it up several times, but everything he said sounded wrong somehow, a man unaware of his core. He gave up eventually, figured that, if they worked together, over time she'd see him for who he truly was, and if they didn't end up working together, well, what difference did it make then what she thought. But perhaps that was a mistake, and a familiar one, too—Avner was never good at telling people what he needed from them, and time and again he realized that once you'd known someone awhile, the dynamic between you was set, plaster that had hardened in its mold.

The hotel room was hoary and mildewed, as he'd suspected it would be for the price he was paying, but Maya didn't seem to mind. She laid her purple backpack on the bed that was closer to the window. When is your meeting? she asked, a tiny businesswoman. She often seemed so much older to him than she really was. Not until tomorrow, Avner said. He pulled out the map the hotel receptionist had given them to find a picture of President Bush in that same paper bag, the words In God We Turst written across it and Welcome to New York State on the bottom. Was this put in there by accident, or was this a gift the hotel was offering new guests? And did no one ever tell them it had a typo? That's the president of the United States, Maya said. Avner nodded. Probably not for long now, he said. Mom calls him President War, Maya said. Avner chuckled. Of course she does, he said. Netta lived and breathed politics, had always wished she could be a full-time activist. She had been taking Maya to protests with her since very early on, which Avner never appreciated but never said anything about. It's not a bad thing, having an American president who's got Israel's back, Avner said. Maya seemed confused. This may have been the first time he addressed anything political with her, and who was he fooling? He didn't care about any of it; one of the best things about leaving Tel Aviv was getting away from those constant and pointless arguments everyone was having. But something was pushing him now to say more. You know, Maymay, he said, Mom and I don't always agree on these things, and I just think you should keep an open mind until you're grown up enough to form your own opinions. I am grown up, Maya said, and he wasn't sure if she was being funny or serious.

A little while later, they went out. I thought we could go see the Empire State Plaza, Avner said. He expected Maya to ask what that was, but she just said Okay. Do you know about the plaza? Avner asked. A tiny nod, and another one. Maya always nodded twice. It's a place with a bunch of buildings and you can see all of Albany from there, she said. Mom and I read about Albany together before I left.

Avner could see them sitting on the living-room couch, Netta entirely absorbed in the girl, as she got whenever she was teaching Maya anything—a siren could go off and she wouldn't hear it—determined to make sure something good came of this needless journey. He did miss Netta, underneath his mess of other feelings, and when Maya was visiting he always missed her more. It was a specific feeling—not the kind that made him reach for the phone, but the kind more based in fantasy: a happy family living in Tel Aviv, a father, a mother, and their eight-year-old daughter. Maybe he's with them on that couch, reading a book. Or perhaps he's in the kitchen, watching them with one eye and a smile, mixing lemon with tahini. Will they ever be that family?

Then he realized, of course, what it meant, this prepping that Netta did. She didn't trust him. He wasn't the dad who'd sit down to read with his daughter, who'd think to look up kids' activities. The only way for Maya to benefit from this trip was for Netta to take care of it herself.

When they reached the plaza, Maya kept looking around with an expression he hadn't quite seen before. Nice, huh? Avner said, and she nodded her two tiny nods. The complex was indeed impressive, and Avner was debating whether he should try to explain what was so special about its architecture.

Did you notice that you can almost see the entire city from here? he asked. Look over there, for example, he said, pointing east. Maya followed his finger with her eyes. You see how these buildings look a little similar to what's around us? This complex *relates* to the city, rather than impose itself on it. Fits in like a piece in a puzzle, even though it's only been around maybe thirty or forty years. See how nothing is blocking the view? It's really quite incredible. Maya nodded, but Avner felt he wasn't being clear. He was never very good at explaining things. Maya kept looking around, and Avner wondered if he should just shut up for a bit, leave her to her thoughts. As with Netta, leaving her alone so often seemed like the right thing to do. But was it? He waited a minute, and another. What are you thinking, Maymay? he asked finally. She wrinkled her nose the way she did when she was embarrassed. It looks like Disneyland, she said, pointing at the other side of the complex, which really did look a lot like the entrance to the Magic Kingdom. This made Avner laugh—the childish simplicity of it, the sweetness, so far from the pompousness of his failed architecture speech—and Maya raised her eyes to look at him, as if asking if he was laughing at her. He wanted to reassure her and was about to say that she was right, it truly did look a lot like Disneyland, when it occurred to him that she'd never been. You're right, Maymay, he said, but how do you know that? I was there a few months ago, Maya said. You were at *Disneyland*? Avner asked, his voice louder than he meant. His daughter had been at Disneyland and he didn't know. His daughter had been in the United States and didn't visit him. It was a gift from Noa's dad for our birthdays, Maya said quietly. Avner felt a familiar tightening in his head, inside his ears. Kleiman took his daughter to Disneyland. And how come Netta didn't mention it, and Maya hasn't, either, until now? Did Netta figure he wouldn't be thrilled and instruct the child to avoid the subject? Would she do that? And didn't she think he needed to be advised before someone—*anyone*, even if it was his close friend—took their daughter on a trip abroad? But he couldn't ask his daughter about any of this, it wouldn't be right, so what he asked was why she was saying "Noa's dad." Didn't she know Kleiman was one of his closest friends? Maya looked at him with wide eyes and said nothing. Perhaps he'd scared her. Never mind, Avner said, and tried to smile, it doesn't matter.

The last time he had talked to Kleiman—it must have been a birthday or some holiday—when the subject of their daughters came up, as it always did, Kleiman talked about how transparent Noa was to him. That was the word he used, *transparent*, as if he could see through her skin. Isn't it freaky? Kleiman was saying. Seeing their little minds figure things out, seeing an idea occur to them for the first time, seeing when they're trying to bluff or pull one over on you . . .

So freaky, Avner said, because he didn't want to tell Kleiman—*Kleiman* of all people—how far his own experience was from that. His daughter was a mystery.

When Maya was about a year old and Noa a newborn, Kleiman came knocking on Avner's door late one muggy summer night. He was loud in the hallway, angry about the heat. Your fucking AC better be on, Kleiman was shouting at the door as Avner was opening it. This was a barking, sweating man facing Avner—quite different from the usual Kleiman, the man nicknamed Buddha in their unit years ago for his calm nature. He stormed in, looking for a button to push. Where is it, where do I turn it on? I need air! The word "air" he shouted even louder. Please be quiet, Avner said; Netta and the baby are asleep. But seconds later Netta was at the end of the hall—blue robe, arms crossed. She stood there, saying nothing; Netta always treated words as if they were in limited supply. He just showed up, Avner started apologizing as if Kleiman weren't in the room, but Netta ignored him and turned to Kleiman. Can I make you some coffee? I think we're done with beer for the night. Kleiman thanked her as if that'd been the point of everything all along, for someone to offer him coffee. This was a special talent of Netta's: people usually wanted what she offered. Netta signaled with her hand, and Kleiman followed her to the kitchen. No one said anything to Avner, but he assumed he should stay in the living room. He'd been struggling for some time to find words that would help his friend, who got a call one day from a woman he barely remembered, telling him she'd just had his baby.

They came out of the kitchen two hours later. Avner was half asleep in his recliner. Help him with the couch, would you? Netta said to Avner, and turned toward the hall that led to their bedroom. Avner and Kleiman opened the sofa bed in silence, as if Netta had pushed both Play and Mute before leaving the room.

The following morning, Netta took Kleiman to the travel agency on Dizengoff Street where she'd worked part-time years before, and where she still had connections. The next day, Kleiman was on a flight to India—back to where he'd spent long months after his military service, an Israeli tradition Avner had always been critical of, believing it only kept people from facing their lives. That evening, Avner overheard Netta on the phone with Noa's mother, offering her help. It was the sort of thing Netta did; she often went out of her way for people she hardly knew. Noa's mother must have mentioned that Netta had a baby of her own to take care of, because Avner heard Netta say, Well, but I've got Avner here. Was Netta only saying what the moment required, or was it possible she actually relied on him in some way? In that first year of Maya's life, he'd only stayed alone with her twice, and for less than two hours each time. He had this horrible fear back then that Maya would somehow die while Netta was gone. He'd mentioned it to Netta once, very early on, and they'd joked about it, but there was something in their laughter, a plea made and heard.

Nine weeks later, Kleiman returned. He seemed to have shed all his angst and anger, left it in India; he was Buddha once again. She's a smart one, your wife, he told Avner.

In the months that followed, something strange happened: Kleiman kept reaching out to Avner for parenting advice. The first time he changed Noa's diaper, the first time he took her to the doctor, the first time she stayed with him overnight. Avner found, amazed, that he knew the answers to most of Kleiman's questions. Since no live demonstrations were ever needed, and since he could always use generic language—not outright *lying*, simply describing what he'd seen Netta do and letting Kleiman infer, perhaps, that it was his own actions he was describing—he was able, it seemed, to be helpful. He had been a father a year longer than Kleiman, after all, and to Kleiman, who seemed oblivious to Avner's own troubles with his little family, that was enough to consider Avner an authority. There was a quality to these talks—a lie repeated until you started believing it—that made them so dear to Avner, and he hid them from Netta, sneaking out to talk or meet with Kleiman as if having an affair. And the affair lasted quite a while, Avner always being one year of fatherhood ahead. But everything changed, of course, when Avner decided to move to New York, a decision the new Kleiman simply couldn't understand. You have a five-year-old here, he whispered to Avner on the balcony of the Tel Aviv apartment, as if reminding his friend of a crucial detail he must have forgotten about, as if forgetting his own history. It may only be for a few weeks, Avner said then.

These days it was Kleiman offering the advice—advice Avner never asked for—and always, it seemed, wanting Avner to confess something. His guilt? How little he knew his daughter? How true that had always been, even before he left? *It's freaky, isn't it, how transparent they are.*

Would you like me to take your picture with Disneyland in the background? Avner asked now. When Maya nodded he remembered he'd left the camera back at the hotel, but his daughter was taking off her backpack, then squatting down and hunting for something. A few seconds later, she was holding a small camera in the shape of a butterfly, stretching her arm up so he could reach. She'd always loved to be photographed. Even back when she was a toddler, Avner remembered, she used to smile and make giggly sounds whenever someone was taking a picture of her. She has a sense of her own beauty, Netta used to say, and then in a lower voice, I hope that never changes. You have your own camera? How great, he said, taking it from her extended hand, looking for the viewfinder. I know what I can do, Maya said suddenly, her voice high with excitement, I can put this in one of those double frames, right next to a real Disneyland one! It will be so funny. I even have a pretty one that Mom took when I was wearing this shirt! Avner pushed the button without meaning to. Mom was in Disneyland, too? he asked. Maya nodded, but her excitement was immediately gone. Was it, like, a group? he asked. Were other people there? Maya shook her head no, her eyes on him. He must be misunderstanding. So it was just Kleiman and Mom, with you and Noa, he said very slowly. Maya nodded. Noa's dad said maybe next time you'll come, too, she said.

Something in Avner was pulling him down now, his body asking to sit or lie for just a moment or two, but it would be so dramatic to do so in the middle of the plaza, and Maya would surely be startled. No, all he needed to do was take her picture; it was a simple task, and he could do it. He held up the camera again. You're not smiling, Maymay, he said in a voice that sounded foreign, the voice of a man he'd never met, and Maya said, Sometimes I like the regular pictures better. What was it about that simple statement? It made him want to close the small distance between them and hug her. But instead he took her picture, tiny and serious, the Disneyland of Albany behind her.

Once they were walking again, there was no pushing the thoughts aside. He wanted to call Netta, ask her point-blank. For once in his life he'd be direct, clear. Would she admit it, assuming there was something to admit? And if she denied it, and he said that, even still, they shouldn't have gone on a trip like that, like *a family* without him, would she understand? Or would she say that they couldn't have afforded it otherwise, which was true, of course, that Kleiman's inviting them was the only way for Maya to go, and didn't he want that for her? Or would she take it even further and finally say what she never had, that he was a bad father for leaving?

He could never—not in all the years they lived together, not since—predict how she'd react to anything. When he started thinking about leaving Israel—when it stopped being a fantasy so secret he seemed to be keeping it even from himself and became something else, hours spent drafting inquiry letters of various kinds—he planned for long months what to say, how to say it. Time and again, he went over different things Netta might say, accuse him of, and he spent days thinking how he'd respond to each. I just need a few months, he was going to say, hoping some part deep down in her that loved him would find compassion for that, because if she could do that for Kleiman, as she had a few years back, why not for him? And maybe that was all it would be—a few months away. He'd focus on his art, get some recognition, figure things out.

When he got the acceptance from the Artists Awake

Association, he stared at it for long minutes, frozen. It was a small thing—a studio space he'd share with other artists probably much younger than himself, a stipend that would buy him a couple dinners a week at best—but it was a nod, someone in New York thinking his work was good. He'd accepted and bought the plane ticket before he talked to Netta, feeling the pull so strong in him and afraid, as he always was, of her effect on him.

He woke up in an empty bed the next morning. That happened often—Netta was an early riser—but he usually knew, even in his sleep, if she was next to him or not. That morning he reached for her to find her gone. And there was something in that moment that gave him the courage he'd been waiting for. He got out of bed and didn't wash his face. He went into the kitchen and didn't say good morning. Any minute, he could lose his nerve. He sat down and said Netta we need to talk I think I need to move to New York for a while I got this residency it's not a lot but it's something I bought a plane ticket. Nothing changed in her face. She kept sitting there looking serene, drinking her coffee and reading the paper. When they first met, Avner was fascinated by how long Netta managed to make one cup of coffee last. She loved her morning ritual and didn't seem to mind her coffee getting cold. Now she took another sip. He hadn't been clear enough. I'm thinking it will be a few months, he said. Maybe some time apart will be good for us. And if I get some people in New York to notice me—maybe get in on some group shows, maybe even find a gallery—

well, it might make all the difference. Right, she said, still reading. He might as well have said, I think we're out of yogurt.

He stayed there a few minutes, sitting across the table and looking at her. This is a woman you can't know, he thought. In the days to come, these words played themselves on repeat in his head, and for reasons he didn't quite understand, they provided comfort. Later, in the New York apartment—his first apartment was a tiny studio in Washington Heights, with hospital-green walls and almost no furniture—he would whisper these words to himself. In the New York winter that awaited him with cold winds that burned his ears and that, being so used to Mediterranean weather, he couldn't help but take personally, he would whisper these words to himself. On New York's long avenue blocks that seemed to be asking out loud when he was going back, when he'd admit he'd made a mistake—he would whisper these words to himself. This is a woman you can't know.

No, he wouldn't call Netta. What would be the point? If she was having an affair with Kleiman, there was nothing he could do about it. Confronting her would only make matters worse. She'd talk to him when she was ready. If there was even anything to talk about, which there might not be. He might be reading too much into it. Things always appeared worse from a distance.

———

At night, back at the hotel (We're home, he'd announced when they came in; he always called wherever he slept *home*), he was going over his portfolio and Maya seemed engrossed in the *Northeast Travel Guide*—Hebrew edition—that he'd brought with him. Gillian had mentioned the Nuweiba series, but you never knew with these people; he might suddenly want to talk about other works entirely. And since none of it came easily to Avner in English, he'd gotten in the habit of looking at his portfolio before any type of meeting, for each work whispering to himself words he might need if he was asked about his intention, or process, or politics. These people often wanted to talk politics.

Did you know people used to live there? Maya was asking suddenly, her voice angry. Where? he asked. Where we went today, that plaza place, she said. It says here—she said, pointing at the book—that people were forced out of their homes to build that place. People used to live there! He leaned toward her, and she handed him the book, marking the relevant section with her finger. He read: "Above the waterline, rising like a spearhead into downtown Albany, stands Nelson Rockefeller's Empire State Plaza, which was built during the 1960s and 1970s, replacing roughly one hundred acres of nineteenth-century buildings (while forcing hundreds of families out of their homes) with a complex including underground parking lots, and decorated with impressive modern art. The view from the observation deck," Avner went on, "looks as if it were specifically designed to make one feel like a triumphant conqueror, looking over the

Hudson winding toward the Adirondacks . . ." He realized he'd gone past the relevant part. This was many years ago, he said to Maya, but her eyes were furious, and he knew his words were wrong. But which words were right? She had always had Netta's uncompromising sense of justice. Or perhaps all children were like that, assuming the world can and should be good. So what if it was a long time ago? Maya asked. They forced people out of their homes! She was looking at him as if he himself had escorted each family out, and her eyes were tearing up. He didn't think she cried anymore. It seemed she stopped doing that years ago, when she learned to talk. Did they use tanks? she asked. How slow he could be sometimes. How had that not occurred to him. Oh, Maymay, he said, it's not the same as back home. It's not what you think. Of course they didn't use tanks. And they probably paid these people, too, for their old houses. It's different in America. Maya looked at him suspiciously. He sighed. Remember what I said earlier, about keeping an open mind with this stuff? That's kind of what I meant. I don't want to go back to that plaza place, Maya said. There's no reason to, Avner said, except we might just have to walk by there tomorrow on our way to my meeting. I don't want to, Maya said. Avner was surprised by her insistence. It was unlike her, to be . . . difficult like that. Okay, he said. I'll figure something out.

Later that night Maya was asleep—on her back, one arm on her stomach and the other on her forehead, her breath loud—and Avner watched her for a while. Every few minutes she'd murmur something and he would try to catch it. It mostly sounded like words in English. He knew she'd been taking lessons; Netta had mentioned it a few times, always emphasizing it, as if he was supposed to say something back—*thank you?*—but still, why would she murmur in English in her sleep? He was probably wrong.

At some point, Avner grabbed his cell phone and sneaked to the bathroom. He sat in an empty bathtub and stared at the small screen. It was early morning in Tel Aviv. Netta might still be asleep. And what would he say? He called Gillian. Maya's practically ready to march into Gaza and throw herself in front of tanks, he told her; I think Netta's been overdoing it with the political zealousness. Gillian laughed. I'm sure you're exaggerating, she said. Maybe, Avner said. They were quiet for a few seconds, until Gillian said, It's late, and her words sounded like a question. I'm sorry, Avner said, should I not have called? No, no, Gillian said, it's totally fine, I'm just surprised. Was that even really what was troubling him, Maya's . . . *politics?* He wasn't sure. But Gillian was always easy to complain to. She never hinted at the fact that he'd *abandoned his child*, never even seemed to think it. He wondered about that sometimes—her absolute empathy, or perhaps it was merely indifference to anything that didn't serve her interest, the art she could sell. I just need to talk to Netta about it, ask her to take it down a notch with the politics, Avner said, though he knew, of course, that he wouldn't. Maya will find her own truth eventually, Gillian said. Gillian didn't understand children, the open-endedness of their minds, how easily they could be manipulated. It's not that simple, Avner said, and they were quiet again for a bit. He wanted to talk to her about Kleiman, about his suspicions. He'd never shared anything real about his marriage. There are many influences in her life, Avner said. Sure, Gillian said. Was she impatient, or was he imagining it? He didn't know what to say next, and Gillian said, You have a big meeting tomorrow, Avner, better try to get some sleep. Had he imagined this whole time that Gillian was . . . open to some other connection between them, that if he ever became available she might be interested? She certainly didn't sound interested now. Yeah, that's really why I called, Avner said. I've been meaning to ask you—can I try to interest this Abe guy in some of my real paintings? I mean, they're never going to sell if no one ever sees them or knows about them. There was a short pause before Gillian said, It's all your *real* work, Avner, and if anything's holding you back it's this kind of thinking. Avner took a deep breath. I know you don't believe they can sell, he said, but, please, tell me the truth: do you think they're good?

Avner . . . was all Gillian said, and then nothing.

The hotel dining room consisted of two small tables, each covered with an oversized plastic tablecloth. Maya and Avner sat there alone, nibbling on stale Danishes. I'm sorry, Avner said; we'll get something better later. It's tasty, Maya said, and took another small bite. He smiled. Better than my

French toast? he asked. Avner was no cook, but he made a better French toast than most—vanilla extract was the secret, and choosing the right bread—and he knew Maya loved it. She giggled. You should teach them how to make it, she said, and maybe then more people would come here! Avner laughed. No way, he said; then I'd have competition! But I will make it for you when we're back home. Maya looked at him with serious eyes suddenly, and he wasn't sure why. Home home? she asked. I meant my apartment, he said. Surely she knew that. But when *are* you coming home? Maya asked, her voice soft and quiet. Netta had explained it all to her, he knew; what did she need to hear?

Maymay, my decision to be here for a while has nothing to do with how much I love you, you know that, right? Maya nodded, but he could tell that wasn't enough. Mom talked to you about it, remember? Maya nodded. But you never did, she said. She was right, of course. That just wasn't how they did things. Netta was so much better at knowing how to manage it all, so much less likely to choose the wrong words, to end up harming Maya even more. Well, he said, what do you want to know? That was probably wrong, he probably wasn't supposed to ask her. I just want to know if it's forever, Maya said.

Did all kids have this skill, this ability to get to the heart of the matter immediately and with few words? I don't know, Maymay, he said. Why not? she asked. He wasn't getting away without giving her some real answers, that much was clear, and perhaps she was truly grown up, as she'd said the day before—at least more than he gave her credit for, and enough for some truth. I was very sad in Tel Aviv, Avner said. He paused for a few seconds. You know that feeling, Maymay, when you do a good job with your homework and the teacher praises you in front of the class? Maya smiled a tiny smile; she did well in school, and he remembered Netta's mentioning her being praised last week. Well, it's a good feeling because praise is important, it's what keeps us going, and I never had that good feeling in Tel Aviv. The galleries and museums over there just didn't like my paintings very much, he said, and shrugged, his shoulders asking her not to feel too bad for him. And in New York they do? Maya asked. Everything is bigger in New York, Avner said, so it takes time, but they do like them more here, yes. He was about to explain that's what the meeting was, too, that he was basically trying to find as many people as he could who would like his paintings, but he paused when he heard the words in his head. It all sounded so . . . pathetic, and surely it wasn't good for a little girl to see her father as pathetic. I like your paintings, Maya said. He put his hand over hers and noticed it was shaking. Thank you, Maymay, he said.

In the waiting room of Abe Chapman's office, everything was large. The brown leather sofas were large, the wooden coffee table was large, the windows—overlooking Madison Avenue, which was nothing like its New York counterpart—were large. Maya had brought a book to keep herself busy, but when Abe's assistant asked if she wanted crayons—holding them up so Maya would understand, asking, *How do you say crayons in Hebrew* but clearly not waiting for Avner to respond—Maya sheepishly nodded. Avner was surprised. He'd always wanted her to draw, wanted to teach her, but she'd had no interest. Such a cutie-pie, the assistant said. She's all right, Avner said, and smiled. He wanted to sit by Maya and watch her draw but had a feeling that would make her self-conscious, so he just stood by the window, awkward and waiting. Shouldn't be long now, the assistant said, and Avner nodded. But twenty minutes later there was still no sign of Abe. Was he in his office with someone, or running late? Avner tended to keep questions to a minimum in such situations. These people were unpredictable. Some wanted to be your best friend, some wanted to humiliate you, so it was hard to know how to be, especially when Gillian wasn't around. He'd gotten pretty good at following her lead, but when he took a meeting without her it was up to him to figure out what the eyes looking at him wanted to see. Except now there were no eyes at all, not yet, and there was Maya, patiently drawing and looking up every few minutes. Didn't he owe it to her, to be more than a forgotten-about appointment in some rich man's waiting room? He took a deep breath. I can't wait much longer, he told the assistant, and his voice sounded hoarse. Oh, I'm sorry, she said, and then in a lower voice, Abe can be so bad with time. I came all the way from New York, Avner said, as if the distance he'd traveled could make Abe materialize. Let me try him again, the assistant said.

She was holding the phone when a heavyset man walked through the front door, his voice immediately filling the space. You must be Avner, he was saying, so sorry to keep you! Oh that's okay, Avner said, and reached his hand out. We were having a nice time.

Avner had assumed Maya would stay in the waiting room with the assistant, but she picked up her crayons when Abe gestured with his arm toward his office and was by Avner's side in seconds. Little one wants to sit in on the meeting? Abe asked, looking at Maya. She doesn't speak a whole lot of English, Avner said, and Abe hit his own forehead with an open hand. Of course! *Ata rotze le yoshev bepgisha?* Maya let out a small giggle. Abe's American Hebrew made her into a boy. There was no way, it seemed, to suggest Maya should wait outside. And maybe that was okay. Maybe it was good for her to see him sell his work, maybe it would give a bit of balance to everything he'd said earlier.

Unlike the waiting room, the office itself was rather naked, a big empty space with only a desk and a couple of chairs. We just moved here a few weeks ago, Abe apologized in his broken Hebrew, we're still waiting on a shipment of furniture from Japan. You don't have to speak Hebrew, Avner tried, but Abe waved his hand. Please, he said, I love it, it's good practice. Maya kept giggling at almost everything he said, which made Avner nervous. Didn't she know it wasn't polite?

So I'm going to be honest with you, Abe said, and tell

you I don't know much about art. But the lovely Miss Gillian tells me that's what this office needs, and I trust that woman. She's the best, Avner said, and smiled. There was a short pause now, the two men looking at each other. Was Avner supposed to say something?

What I do know quite a bit about, Abe said, leaning forward, and *care* about—deeply—is *Eretz Israel.* Is that something we have in common, Avner?

Avner had met people like Abe before, staunch supporters of Israel who considered it their job to make everyone else support Israel right along with them. Yes, Avner said, of course. Oh, it's not *of course*, Abe said, not these days, sadly. And not when talking to an Israeli who's no longer living in Israel. Abe smiled a wide smile. Was this man seriously judging him? This man who at best volunteered at some kibbutz for a year, who certainly never served in the army? This was unusual. Avner was used to questions about Israel, about his politics, about his politics in relation to his art. And to a degree, he'd always rationalized, that was fair. They wanted to know what they were buying, and often these were not people who knew what they were looking at when they looked at a painting. But he'd never been criticized or shamed in any way for leaving Israel. Most of the time, all he needed to do was talk about his military days and their eyes would light up.

I left Israel for personal reasons, Avner said, glancing in Maya's direction. She was sitting on the floor and seemed engrossed in her drawing, but she could be misleading in this way. None of my business of course, Abe said, switching back to English and still smiling, but seems to me personal reasons should have kept you from leaving, if anything.

Avner shifted in his chair. What the fuck was going on today? Maybe Abe, too, would like to know if he was staying in New York forever. Avner's face must have been showing his discontent, because after a few seconds Abe said, I apologize if that was too blunt, Avner—I truly don't mean to offend. Only to see if we have a good . . . rapport, so to speak. If we see eye to eye on things. I hope you don't take this the wrong way, Avner said, but why does it matter? If you like my paintings, you like my paintings. It was the sort of thing you weren't supposed to say, of course, the sort of thing Gillian would never let him ask if she were here. But Abe didn't seem surprised. That's a fair question, he said, and then paused—perhaps to think, perhaps for effect; Avner couldn't tell. Let me first say, Abe finally said, that I'm looking at getting about twelve pieces. Two for each office, three for the conference room, three for the foyer. Okay, Avner said, doing his best to keep his voice steady. Gillian never mentioned twelve anything. Usually they looked at a few and chose one if he was lucky. Selling twelve works—he could never do the math in his head while talking, but it meant he'd be okay, more than okay, for a good while. He'd be able to see Maya much more often. He'd be able to take her to Disneyland.

So to be honest, Abe said, that's part of the answer to your question—it's a considerable investment, and I'd like to know who's benefitting from it. Avner nodded. Perhaps that was all he needed to do, perhaps he could nod his way to the end of the meeting. But also, Abe said, shaking his head lightly and pursing his lips as if not quite sure how to put it—I'm always . . . on the lookout. For the right kind of people. For people who I may *collaborate* with on different projects. Avner had no idea what Abe was talking about, but suddenly felt like he was being vetted for something. What kind of projects? Avner asked. In a minute, Abe said, but let me ask you this first, Avner: what's your competitive edge? My competitive edge? Avner repeated, and immediately wished he hadn't. Abe said, Sorry, I'm used to thinking in business terms; if you think of yourself as a one-man venture, if this is a value proposition—what's your edge? You mean as an artist? Avner asked. Sure, Abe said. And Avner started to explain about his real work then, how it captured the relationship between man and urban space, but Abe stopped him. I must have not explained myself very well, he said, his hand raised in the air between them. And he went on then to answer his own question. Avner's competitive edge was that he was Israeli. Or, more specifically, that he was an Israeli and an artist and relatively young. He could appeal to some people, important people, who were afraid of the word Zionism.

I'm not only a Zionist, Avner, Abe said, I'm an *active* Zionist. Being Jewish and being Zionist should be synonymous. It stands to reason, doesn't it? And yet in some circles it's a become a word people hesitate to use. Do you know why that is, Abe asked, but didn't wait for Avner to respond.

Self-hate, he announced, if you ask me. Self-hate is what's keeping so many Jews, so many *Israelis*, from supporting Israel. It's so sad, when you think about it, Abe said, bringing one hand to his chest in a gesture so preposterous Avner struggled not to look away. So much hatred has been directed at the Jewish people over the years, and Israel was supposed to be the answer to that. Instead, Abe said, it's become the main excuse for many people to hate Jews, and for many Jews to hate themselves. Don't you agree?

This was a familiar feeling, his arm being pulled on in this way. It was the same with Netta—the convictions were different, but the pull the same. People who believed they had the answers were like paparazzi—so focused on getting the shot they wanted, so narrow in their aim.

Of course, Avner said, self-hate never leads anywhere good. If this idiot wanted to buy his affirmation for thousands and thousands of dollars, Avner would sell it. There, I agree with you. Now pay up. Terrific, Abe said, terrific, but his expression seemed troubled, and he paused before he continued. Because the thing is, now more than ever, it is crucial for Jews to stand together, be united. Avner wasn't sure why "now more than ever," but he knew Abe believed what he was saying, believed, probably, that any moment now Israel might cease to exist. That was a fundamental difference between Israelis and American Jews: Israelis, at least those born after '48, born into the reality of Israel as a state, could never imagine any other reality. And whether they were right or wrong, what Avner had come to recognize through his time in New York was the comfort that belief provided. American Jews didn't seem to share that comfort; most of them, at least the ones Avner met, seemed to believe every time they opened the paper there might be an ad announcing the demise of the Jewish State. And Avner often felt guilty in these conversations, because what a luxury it was, taking the existence of anything for granted.

He glanced in his daughter's direction. I agree, Avner said to Abe, and smiled; Jews should support one another. But again, what . . . projects are we talking about? Abe laughed. See, that's why I love Israelis, he said—never let you get away with anything. But I truly wasn't talking about anything in particular, Avner, not yet at least. Generally speaking, I'd love to invite you to some events, some galas. You can sell your pictures, talk to some people. How does that sound? Paintings, Avner said, although he knew that was petty, not the thing to say right now, but he couldn't help it—I'm not a photographer. Of course, of course, Abe said, as I told you, I'm no big mavin when it comes to this stuff. Avner nodded, tried to smile. One more thing, though, Abe said. If we're going to do all this, I'd like to make sure the . . . paintings carry that message. It seems to me it's all a bit . . . open to interpretation, don't you think? I mean, I look at those gorgeous pictures of Sinai, but all it says is *Nuweiba, 1980.* What does that mean?

It means it's a painting of what Nuweiba looked like in 1980, Avner said. Yes, yes, Abe said. But you know what I'm saying, Avner. This was Israeli territory back then, but months later it was given to Egypt. Given *back* to Egypt, Avner said.

For peace, Abe said slowly, looking straight into Avner's eyes. Because that's all Israel's ever wanted.

Maya wasn't drawing anymore. She was looking up now, looking serious. What was she able to pick up on from the Hebrew and English mix they were speaking? All I'm proposing is that the subtitle be a bit more accurate, Abe said. Something like *Neviot in Sinai, Israel, 1980.* A gentle reminder of Israel's many sacrifices.

Avner felt Maya's eyes on him. She probably didn't understand what Abe was saying, what he was asking. And even if she did, Avner could explain it later. He'd say something like, This man loved my paintings so much he wanted to be part of them. He should be able to avoid the politics of it altogether, that wasn't the point.

Abe was still talking. With some of the other pictures, he was saying now, changes might have to go a bit further, but I'm sure we can figure it out. He paused and looked at Avner. Avner knew what he was talking about—some of the older paintings had racier text, for sure, and he'd be lying if he didn't admit they were inspired by Netta's politics more than his own. And yet the paintings were what they were, the text part of the work. Could he really . . . change them? This was only a test, that much was clear. This man didn't care about Avner's art any more than he cared about Palestinians dying in Gaza. Neither was real to him in the full sense of the word. But if Avner was willing to "edit" his paintings, that would prove he was the kind of man Abe and his friends wanted to . . . bring into the fold.

Avner felt the sweat on his face. Was it visible? He didn't have it in him to stand up to this man, say no to all that money, the connections, everything that might befall him if he went along. You never knew where things might go if you befriended these types of people, people who sat on boards, who had halls of libraries named after them. Maybe he'd just start this way, as this puppet Abe wanted to make of him, but once he met some people who did care about art, he'd explain that these paintings of Israel were a different phase and he was doing new things now. He'd show them his real work. And who knew what could happen then. That's how people made it in New York. It's not a problem, Avner said. Abe smiled. All right, then, he said. I'm sure you'll need some time to do that, so how about we meet again in a couple months and go from there? For a few seconds, the two men looked at each other. So that was that.

Abe got up and shook Avner's hand. Then he turned to Maya. Your daddy's a smart man, he said, and Avner felt his muscles tighten. He turned to Avner again. Don't be . . . shy about your views, Avner, all right? Can you teach your daddy to be less shy? Abe asked Maya. My dad isn't shy, Maya said. Abe laughed. She's feisty, the little one, he said, and Israeli, no doubt. Avner tried to chuckle, but what came out of him sounded more like a cough.

They left the building in silence, walked slowly. He needed to call Gillian to give her the update, but he couldn't. She'd make him feel better, but somehow he wasn't sure that was what he wanted.

I didn't like that man, Maya said. How come? Avner asked; he tried to sound casual but was bracing himself for a difficult conversation. He was fat, Maya said. This caught Avner unprepared, and he chuckled. Maymay, he said, that's not very nice. But it was too late; she was giggling and blowing air into her cheeks, marking a fat stomach with her arms. I am Abe, she was saying, trying to imitate the walk of a heavy man, I am so fat I can hardly move. She was trying to keep a straight face as Fat Abe, but she kept giggling, and Avner couldn't help but laugh. He'd never seen this side of her. Was his daughter playful? Was *Netta's* daughter playful? Now Avner was walking funny, too. I am Fat Abe, he said. I am always late because I walk so slow.

Surely he'd heard her laugh that way before? There was something so pure in that sound, water trickling down a pond.

A little while later, he felt a tickle in his left palm. It took him a few seconds to realize it was Maya's hand trying to make its way into his. He opened his palm, took his daughter's hand. Soon, they'd arrive.

THIS WAY I DON'T HAVE TO BE

1. Waiting for the Eye Doctor in Tel Aviv

A man is playing with his son. He seems too young to be the boy's father, and yet he clearly is. Dad, Dad, the boy keeps saying, leaving no room for doubt. A stack of cards is the centerpiece of the action. They are playing a game called How Far Can You Blow the Card.

Are you the last one? a woman with a baby asks me, and before I have time to answer, she starts telling me what happened this morning. This morning, she says with excitement that seems inappropriate, I suddenly noticed this thing in my baby's left eye. See? See? she asks again when I fail to respond. I don't see anything. There is nothing to see. I nod. Oh my God, you see it, too, she says; do you think it's bad, do you think it's something really bad? I really don't, I say, subtle sarcasm in my voice, and the man turns his eyes from his son—turns his eyes from his son!—and looks at me. He smiles. I smile back. We are obviously the sophisticated ones among the people waiting for the eye doctor. Is he flirting with me?

An old woman comes out of the doctor's room. I need to go in again in fifteen minutes, she announces. No one responds. I'm going to go now, she tells me, but I'll be back in time, you'd better not try to cut in front of me. She seems to dislike me, but I have no idea why. Whore, she hisses before she leaves. Hey, hey, the man tells her. My knight. She's just an old crazy woman, I tell him, to show that I don't care and to remind him of our shared sophistication.

The eye doctor's clinic is situated in an old building in the south of Tel Aviv, not far from where I grew up. There is nothing wrong with my eyes, but these routine checkups are a good way to keep busy when I visit; too much free time makes parents ask questions like, Anybody special in your life now? And, Would you like us to come visit you in New York in the spring?

Inside, there's a waiting room with pictures of the human eye like you've never seen it. No windows. Outside, where we all wait on an oblong-shaped balcony atop a stairwell, the marble floor makes squeaky sounds every time someone moves, and the peeling paint on the banister looks like old cake batter. My eyes follow the woman down the stairs and onto the small street. She constantly looks like she might fall, but she doesn't, and I taste guilt in my throat when I notice my disappointment. If she turns right and walks straight, she'll hit the flea market. If she turns left and walks north, bookstores and small coffee shops will be the slow-moving background of her tour. I stretch my body in an attempt to see her choice, but she is gone.

The baby is staring at me. I smile at him or her. It is still staring. The mother is making ridiculous sounds, trying to get its attention. It won't stop staring at me. You know, she says finally, studies show that babies tend to focus on beautiful people. Thank you, I say.

Is she flirting with me?

You want to look at the beautiful girl, don't you, don't you now. You're already a little man, aren't you. Yes, you are, oh yes, you are.

Score! the man's son shouts out. Way to go, Oren, the man says, and winks at me, letting me know he didn't really lose to a five-year-old. He's just being a good father. High five, he says, and raises his hand. But you lost, the boy says, keeping his hands to himself. It's okay to be happy for somebody else's victory, Oren, the man says, glancing at me to make sure I'm listening. He obviously has the whole fatherhood thing nailed down. Nobody says high five anyway, the boy says, only old people. The man looks sad. Or amused.

There's some confusion as to who should go in first, the woman with the baby or a woman in a dress that looks like a blanket. What about you, blanket woman says to the man with the son. It's all good, my knight says. Take it easy, ladies, that's what Fridays are for; we'll all get in at some point. He's clearly not the typical Israeli; there is no aggressiveness in him, no sense of urgency. I think, That should be interesting in bed.

I'm not a baby, but I focus on beautiful people too, he tells me on his way out. It's not a great line, but I smile anyway. The son is right there. He seems to be concentrating on his cards. Is he okay? I ask the man. Minor infection, he says, and pats the boy's hair. Right, big guy? The child doesn't seem to hear his father's question. Life, to him, is very much about those cards. The man isn't wearing a wedding ring, and I'm trying to fool myself, like this: Maybe he's divorced, he could be divorced. But the truth is that Israeli men often don't wear their wedding rings, and I know that he is in fact married, the way I always know immediately when I look at a man. It's a feeling that comes over me, a tickle of excitement that never lies. It starts behind my belly button, then spreads. I think, Be strong be strong be strong. But I am not strong. He hands me the doctor's business card, and I write my number on the back, smiling. Better not waste time, I tell him, handing him back the card; I live in New York and am here for only two more days.

2. Going Back

He takes me to an area outside of Tel Aviv where signs claim a beautiful mall will soon dazzle every passerby; for now, there is nothing but sand dunes. His car is an old Subaru; he parks it and tries to recline, but the seat screeches its resistance. When he wins this small battle, I see clearly that he's a man who can't leave his wife behind; I know the type, and I'm disappointed. Invisible wives make men's bodies seek only a sense of accomplishment, not pleasure. When he climaxes, I am a magician halfway through her show, with a passed-out audience. Then he sighs, relieved that it's behind us. Reaching for the Kleenex on the tiny dashboard, he asks, Did you come?, but doesn't seem to expect a response. I roll down the window and let the sandy Israeli air tickle my nostrils until I sneeze.

I call Lizzie right when I get back; it's a transatlantic call, but I tell myself my parents must not mind the charge, judging by how often they call me when I'm in New York. I say, Liz, I fell off the wagon. She says, I knew it. She's upset, and probably disappointed, which is sort of why I called; this way I don't have to be. I can hear one of the Lizzies thinking: She's really hopeless, this one. That's always the scariest moment, and it stretches out like a whole life, a life in which I'm alone with my problems. I know better, I know Lizzie would never give up on me, I know to wait for the other Lizzie; but there's always that moment, and that voice that says, But what if. Finally she says, Are you ready to work hard. It doesn't sound like a question, and her voice is gruff. I say, Of course, of course. But the truth is, I can't feel it. I can't feel my readiness to work hard. When are you coming home? she asks, although she knows the answer.

On the plane, on the way back, a man is sitting next to me. His wedding ring flickers. I think, By now, what's the difference if I do or don't? Then I think, Be strong be strong be strong. And he's not even good-looking. But then I look at the ring again and think, This has gotten so bad that clearly I'm going to clean up when I get back, and so what's the difference, really, if I have a little fun right now? It doesn't matter, when you think about it. I close my eyes and imagine us in the tiny lavatory, a voice-over announcing impending turbulence. Ooh, he says. Apparently, the turbulence turns him on. Ooh, I say to his neck, and then fake another one, ooh.

Back in New York, the world speeds up again and I'm left behind. I sleep for two days, and then it's time for work. I am a grief counselor. Israelis consult me about their grief, and I offer efficient ways of coping. The Israeli government pays me to tell Israelis Living Abroad that if their son died in a suicide bombing they should stick to a rigid sleep regimen and drink green tea every morning. When I moved to New York to run away from my addiction (I was under the impression then that my drug was exclusively *Israeli* married men), the counseling job was supposed to be temporary, until I figured out what I wanted to do; but it turned out not to be temporary at all, maybe because, like Lizzie says, nothing ever is. I get a lot of death-related grief, but sometimes more interesting cases, too, like people who don't feel at home in New York but don't want to go back, or like that woman whose cats kept dying; she adopted a new kitty every time as an affirmation of her trust in the universe, and every time the universe failed her. Any grieving person who proves their grief to be related to the situation in Israel is entitled to twelve hours of free counseling. Put the word *free* in the title and you're guaranteed long lines of eager Israelis.

Every visit takes a few weeks to shake off, and this one isn't any different; skipping back and forth between my two worlds feels like some maniac kid keeps pushing Reset on a computer that controls my behavior. I'm more aggressive, more impatient with my clients. I find it impossible to hold the door for the person behind me, or to smile at a stranger on the street just because we are both human beings. People don't do these things in Israel, and it takes me several weeks every time to remember why I should. Americans say New Yorkers are rude, but I think it all depends on your point of reference. Another difference: pacing. There is rage and rudeness in Israel, but they move around confidently, knowing nothing is ever going to change. In New York people run and run and run, because change is absolutely possible, if only they run fast enough to catch it.

On my fifth day back, Lizzie and I go out. At the bar, she follows my eyes to a man in a gray sweater. He's alone, and we can't see his left hand from where we sit, but I feel the tickle and know, and because of me Lizzie knows, too. Lizzie is an addiction expert; she's helped many people and even invented her own method for adults whose addiction is not 12-steps compatible. There's a clinic in Vermont that practices her method, and they call it the Brinn Method, because Brinn is Lizzie's last name. Mention the word *clinic*, or *method*, or *Vermont*, and there's no escaping a ten-minute lecture titled Why I Am Great, by Lizzie Brinn.

I make fun of her sometimes (though not often to her face), but the truth is, she's my map to the treasure; a day without her and I start to think maybe there's no treasure at all.

Lizzie always says, You really are a special case. By that she means I'm more messed up than most. Every time she says it, I feel like somebody put pride and anxiety in a one-shot glass and said, Drink. Now, at the bar, she says it again and adds, But I have a new idea. I want to say, Can we talk about it another time? but I ask, What is it? Lizzie says, We have to do something drastic and dramatic because nothing we do seems to stick with you. I say, I'm listening. Lizzie says, You can skip work next Tuesday, right? Because I'm thinking Monday night will be good for this, so you'll need the morning after for sleep. I say, Sure. Lizzie says, I'll need you to go over everything you own, absolutely everything.

I'll tell you what to look for, she says, but I'll need you to be thorough, ruthless, brave. Can you do that? she asks, and before I have a chance to answer, she says, Tell me if you can't, I need to know now if you're not up to it. There is urgency in her voice, which makes me uneasy, but I still say what I know she wants to hear. What choice do I have, Lizzie? Her eyes nod at me.

At the end of the night I walk home; the bar is exactly six blocks north of my apartment and south of Lizzie's. I think about the man in the gray sweater, I think about going back. He was still there when we left, sitting on his stool and drinking slowly, deep in thought like he was contemplating different ways to stop some war. Like possibly he was briefing the president in the morning. It appeals to me, this sense of duty in a man.

I think how sex with him would feel. I think how his face would look in that one moment that matters, the moment that relieves my guilt of its weight, the moment I wait for. I always look them in the eye throughout, so as not to miss my moment, and that can be tricky, because they mostly try to avoid the intimacy of eye contact. I wait, and then suddenly it's there, passing through them like a wave. In that moment, their entire lives turn to air—their mothers, babying them too much in the early years, or leaving on the eve of their thirteenth birthday to reunite with a salesman in Kentucky, or fighting cancer for years, being *so damn brave*; their fathers, the memory of snow caves, of absence, of Camel Lights; their wives, that moment when their eyes first locked through Halloween masks, and this morning, the way she turned her face away in bed, so many gentle moments, so many small heartbreaks; and their children, those scary hours at the hospital, and the first time the baby girl said Daddy, or Home, or Clementine, and they realized the true meaning of the word *devotion.* It all disappears. What's left is something from years ago, an idea of the men they wanted to be, long abandoned. For one brief moment, they go back in time, they make different choices, they are different men. And my body is the time machine that takes them there.

I keep walking, I don't go back to the bar, simply because right now I am able not to. I want to feel something like accomplishment, the conquering of weakness, but I don't. I feel numb. It's colder than it should be this time of year, and I'm drunk and can't wait to get home. I am thinking Get home get home get home, but when I get home I don't feel like going in. I imagine opening the door, turning the light on; I imagine my blue pajamas, my empty bed. I can actually see it and feel it, because that's something Lizzie and I have been working on for a long time: Visualization. Through the help of Visualization, I become convinced that I don't want to go into my apartment. I call Lizzie from the hallway, and I whisper because I don't want to wake any neighbors up, and if they're already up, I don't want them to hear me; I wouldn't think much of someone in my situation. Lizzie says, I don't see what the problem is. I say I just don't want to go in. She says, But why? I say I just don't, it feels wrong, I know I'll be sad. Lizzie is quiet for a few seconds, and then she says, Are you going to fuck somebody now, is that it? It's harsh, and I can hear the three shots of vanilla Stoli in her words. I say, I'm *not* going to fuck anyone tonight, that's the whole point. Then I think I hear someone in the background, but I don't ask her about it.

After we hang up the phone I'm still unable to go in, and the walls are dancing, so I sit down. From the floor, things are looking up. The hallway feels steadier, and I think, This is not so bad. I stay there, on the welcome mat by the door to my apartment, and I fall asleep. When I wake up a few hours later, there is daylight, and opening my front door seems easy. I walk in and feel nothing except the need to shower, the need to change clothes, the need to go to work. What was my problem last night? I think in the shower. I was *drunk*, I think, and I giggle to myself and the water giggles back.

3. The Bonfire

Monday night, Lizzie honks the horn for me to come downstairs. The car is Oz's. Oz is a guy who used to be addicted to cucumbers—used to eat a few dozen every day, throw up, and start all over. Lizzie helped him, and now they're fuck buddies. Once, Lizzie and I went to Six Flags (stages six and seven in the Brinn Method, Getting in Touch with the Child Within and Experiencing Danger in a Safe Environment), and there was some kind of problem with one of the roller coasters. At the top of the man-made mountain we sat, waiting, and talked about Oz, because he and Lizzie had just had sex for the first time the night before. I said something mean or cynical about his addiction, and Lizzie got very upset. She said, I'm not supposed to discuss this with you, but Jesus, can't you figure it out? I mean, clearly it's a phallic thing, and I'll just say this: he had a very rough childhood. I felt stupid. You of all people, she said, and I really hoped she wouldn't finish the thought. Then she said, All you addicts are the same; you all think you're better, your addictions are sophisticated and complicated and other people's are beneath you. There was something in Lizzie's voice then that made it easy to imagine her one day saying, I don't think I can help you anymore. I've never said a bad word about Oz since.

I put my bags in the backseat and get into the car. It smells funky, but I don't say anything because it's Oz's car. Instead, I say, Why did you honk, you could have buzzed or called. I know the answer: Lizzie likes to honk. She knows I know the answer, so she just honks again and smiles at me like a wink. I grab her honking hand, but not too strong, and say, Shhhh. Lizzie glances at the side mirror and starts to pull out. She asks, Do you have everything? and I nod but she can't see me so she asks again. Yes, I say; I have everything.

Lizzie puts a crumpled green Post-it in my hand and asks, What exit does it say? Lizzie can write tomes on Post-its in her tiny, compressed handwriting, but I've always been good at deciphering it. I read: *Take the Belt Parkway to exit 6. Head south on Cropsey Avenue to West 17th Street. KeySpan Park and the Parachute Jump will be in front of you on Surf Avenue. Metered parking is available along most streets.* Fuckers, Lizzie says, they don't want you to park close to the beach; but we'll see. Who, the evil powers of Yahoo Maps? I say. No, it's from their website, Lizzie says; there's an official Coney Island website. Well why'd you copy it if you weren't going to follow the instructions anyway, I ask; for some reason this annoys me, and I fantasize about nudging Lizzie's shoulder hard so she'll lose control of the car. Maybe I'll grab the wheel and save us. Maybe we'll swerve, fast and sharp like on a Six Flags ride.

Lizzie looks at me like she can see my thoughts. We can park exactly where they want us to, she says, and carry all your shit for two miles, or we can park where we need to park, and assume the police have higher priorities this time of night; what's your pleasure? You know I get bitchy when I'm nervous, I say, just ignore me. She does.

At Coney Island, the air is smoky and salty and the sand looks like ashes. Lizzie walks confidently past a few small bonfires: schoolkids, new lovers. I follow her to a secluded area behind a large Dumpster that seems misplaced. Lizzie says, You can leave your stuff here. Then, for about thirty minutes, we go back and forth from our spot to the car, where there's a trunkful of planks. Then Lizzie starts the fire.

While I'm taking everything out of the bags, Lizzie says, You really mean it this time. Lizzie's instruction was Bring everything your addiction finds inspiring. So I packed bags and bags of inspirations: everything the men had ever given me, pictures where we look happy, private journals with too much truth. Then I thought, Do better do better do better, so I added DVDs we watched together, the lace bra that opens from the front—anything that held a memory.

I'm happy that Lizzie has noticed my effort, and I say, I'm done, Liz, I'm done; no more married men. Then I say *I'm done* one more time, to make sure. By now the bonfire is something that can harm. Lizzie starts ripping things, and with her eyes she says, You do the same. I do. I know we have to make everything small before we burn it; one of the principles of the Brinn Method is Graduality, which means breaking down any Significant Action into several mini-actions whenever possible. When we're done she says, I can't do any burning for you. I start feeding the fire—carefully at first, but then it gets wild. I'm jumping in the air, attacking the bonfire from all directions, screaming. The fire eats away at my fantasies, and the smoke that it feeds back to the air feels sober.

When Lizzie asks if I'm ready, I assume she means am I ready to go home, and I say yes. She says, Then we should get started. I give her a look that says I don't understand, and she says, Listen to me: What's the one thing we've been ignoring all this time, the missing variable in your addiction's equation? What's our oversight? (A big part of the Brinn Method is finding oversights.) I say I don't know. Lizzie looks at me. Think, she says. I can't think. I say I don't know. She says, The kids. I say, The kids? and she repeats, The kids; most of your men had kids, but we never bothered with that, it seemed immaterial. That's our oversight! she declares, and I can tell she's been waiting for this moment for days.

Lizzie reaches for one of the bags, takes out a big brown envelope, and starts handing me photographs. I'm sitting on the sand and she's standing close to me, studying my reactions. In the photographs, random children play or cry, unaware of the camera. I look up at Lizzie and say, I don't get it. What's not to get? she asks; these are the kids. I still don't quite understand, but then I see him—the kid with the cards, from the eye doctor, only he looks older than I remember, and there are no cards in this picture. Instead, there's a dog, and he seems to be talking to it. I think, This can't be right. I look at Lizzie, then at the picture again. Lizzie looks pleased, almost smug. I say nothing for a few minutes, and stare at the blackness of the water. Lizzie is giving me the time that I need, because she thinks I'm making progress.

Then she says something about talking to the photographs, apologizing to the children, but I can't really hear her. I get up, shake the sand off. Where did you get these? I ask her. I have my ways, she says, and smiles. I look her straight in the eye. Where did you get these? I ask again. Now she can see that there is no progress at all. What's your problem? she asks; you know how much effort, not to mention money, I had to put in to get these? You think it's easy? I don't think it's easy at all, I say; I think it's fucked up. Lizzie looks at me. Are we regressing back to Resistance, she asks, is that what's happening? I want to know how you got these, I tell her for the third time, but this time there's more weakness than threat in my words.

The soles of my feet are numb now. I can't stand, and I don't want to sit back down. I need to go home, I tell Lizzie. Not before we do this, she says. I shake my head no, slowly. Then I look right at her and say, I don't give a fuck about these kids. I didn't make them. Get their fathers to apologize to them, not me.

There is madness in her eyes and I think she might hit me, but she says nothing and then puts the photographs back in the envelope, the envelope back in the bag.

On the drive back to the city we are silent, but when we get to my block Lizzie says, You weren't ready; it's my fault. All of a sudden I have the urge to ask her if she called Oz to come over the other night after the bar. I want to suggest that maybe she has problems of her own, and that maybe she should focus on those for a while. But I figure whatever I say, I'm likely to regret it in the morning. When I'm about to enter my building, Lizzie honks, and I know she wants me to turn around and smile; I walk in without looking back.

4. Grief

Two weeks later, Lizzie and I are splitting a tuna sandwich and a lemonade on St. Marks, and she's holding the lemonade and taking fast, short sips, because she never had any siblings and isn't good at sharing. I let her, and focus on the tuna sandwich until she says, Hey, leave some for me. I look at her and feel the itch of confession. Lizzie's way of dealing with the bonfire night has been to pretend it went well; even without completing the evening's full program, as far as she's concerned, we were ultimately successful. She's been carefully constructing her sentences around *now that you're clean*. Soon, I know, if I don't stop the charade, she will start planning my 100 Free Days Celebration. I say, These past few weeks . . . you don't know the whole story. Then I ignore her face and tell her about the man on the plane. She's taking a deep breath. And since the bonfire? she asks. I tell her there have been two men since the bonfire, even though there's only been one; I need her to lose hope. One was a grief client, I say, the other a regular at the coffee shop I go to who told me he was getting married in three days. Lizzie says, Okay, okay, and nods slowly many times, until it gets irritating. I say, I think the worst part is, I don't regret it. Lizzie gives me the Lizzie look. I say, I just don't, and shrug.

A woman comes into my office. She has beautiful eyes, but where they meet the rest of her face you can see fatigue. She says, I think I'm addicted to my grief. Grief is a very addictive substance, I say. We are not supposed to say things like that, but I don't care. She seems surprised, like she expected me to say something else entirely, or maybe just offer her a glass of water. She asks about studies, and I understand: she wants printed data, black ink on stapled paper. Everyone does. I say, Suppose some research has been conducted, suppose proof exists that grief is one of the most dangerous drugs out there, that tens of thousands of Israelis abuse it every day; do you really think the government would let that information out? She looks at me like she doesn't understand, but I know that she does. You have to go slowly with these people; they are not always ready to know what they already know.

We are quiet for a few seconds until suddenly she says, Everyone is an addict, then. My clients often exaggerate, once they see my point. Well, not *everyone*, I reply. I want to focus on her personal grief now, but she repeats her statement, and there is conviction in her tone, like she has slammed some door I can't see: Everyone is an addict. I say, Addiction is a serious matter; you are belittling it when you put it this way. If anything can be an addiction, she says, then everyone is an addict. Please stop saying "everyone is an addict," I say. I should point out the flaws in her logic, but somehow I can't. Instead, my brain fills with words that can hurt her, words like *wrinkles* and *faded*. She smiles and looks at the wall behind me, and I get a strange feeling, like part of me has been sleeping this whole time. I turn around to see what it is she's looking at, but it's all white. I say, I think our time is up.

When I leave the office I'm shaking. I call Lizzie three times. Finally she picks up and she hears the trembling and she says What's wrong, what's wrong. I say, I think I'm done. Lizzie says, You've said it before. I say, No, I mean I'm done trying. Lizzie says nothing and I say, Liz, it's not going away and I'm spending my life trying to change my life instead of living it. But what else can you do, Lizzie says very quietly, like a secret. I don't know yet, I say, but whatever it is, I have to do it on my own. We can figure something out, she says, just because the bonfire didn't work it doesn't mean— Liz, I say, that's the whole point; no more we can figure it out. *I* need to figure it out. The last words come out louder than I intended. Lizzie is quiet again. I am walking faster now, and I feel like I can walk forever, all the way to Israel and back. I know that I can't, but the thought makes me light, and when I realize Lizzie is no longer on the line I put the phone in my pocket. I am almost running now, and it stops the shaking. I look at my legs; I can see my muscles working, my feet landing neatly on the ground every time to keep me from falling. I think, We are a team, my legs and me. I think, I am strong.

STAND STILL

In the office where we worked, a windowless kitchenette stood at the end of a hall; in it, an espresso machine proudly rose from a countertop made of cold marble. One day, we craved the coolness of the marble, the heat of bitter caffeine, at the exact same time. In the kitchenette, we reached for the knob, then for the nozzle. Our hands touched, our skins tickled. The machine roared, let out steam. Still, we laughed it off. We said *Excuse me.* We returned to our desks and emulated the motions of coworkers. You see, we had both offered our freedom to other people long ago, and they'd accepted.

The next day it happened again. And again.

One of us, though we are not at liberty to say who, began to suspect the presence of a powerful force.

For a while, only a few people shared our secret. After nodding at these people over glasses of stale iced tea, as they advocated for restraint and touched the tips of our shoulders, we'd often find gray spots under our skin. They looked like bruises. We knew what they were. We had no escape, the force was reminding us, lest our friends' words fool us.

Once, we bought a special detergent, legal in our state only for the use of veterinarians with pure intentions. Over the small kitchenette faucet we hunched, as one of us tried to scrub the other clean. We squeezed grainy matter out of green tubes. It didn't work.

What could we do? We said goodbye to our spouses, affectionately kissed them on the cheek, avoided their eyes as we reached for the door. We left many items behind. We held on to our keys. Anything else, we knew, would be too cruel.

We had a plan: separate apartments. It's the difference between cooking to surprise a lover, and cooking because your lover is hungry, we said. But every morning we'd wake up together, unable to remember the previous night. Unwittingly, we started using the same Laundromat. At the grocery store, we found ourselves aware of each other's preferences, shopping for two. *Why am I choosing semisoft tomatoes?* one of us would think; *I always said soy can't be milk*, the other would mumble, carton in hand. Soon, the elaborate ring of keys felt heavy in our pockets, and the clinking sound it made annoyed us.

We found a house with leaves on every window. We were undressing each other so often that some days putting clothes back on seemed a waste of time. We appreciated the trees for this reason—they made it so we could be naked and believe ourselves unobserved. Except, that is, for the force, which, we assumed, if it wanted to watch us would not be deterred by greenery.

After a while, one of us—and it truly doesn't matter who—had a crisis in the family. We have different memories of what the crisis was—one of us believes a beloved aunt fell ill, while the other remembers it clearly as a sibling's drug problem. What is not in dispute is that solving the crisis involved travel and an extended stay, and that while one of us was packing, the other felt terrified, and thrilled.

While one of us was away, the other started working long hours, creating expectations in the office that later proved difficult to amend. We were not working in the same office by then, but we were still in the same business—figuring out if companies needed to get bigger or smaller—and we both understood the nature of that business.

We still talk about that trip often—it seemed to take something away from us, and perhaps give something in return.

We admit that freely, often over a glass of wine, and one of us tickles the other's knee to remind us we are still playful.

Over time, we got in the habit of taking our own clothes off when needed. When you undress yourself, you have plenty of time to close a curtain, and so the trees grew less important. But we still loved the green on our windows, especially when the yellow of the sun mixed with it a particular way. Such views were hard to come by in our state—most living quarters were overlooking other living quarters. We fully accepted that our love for our windows meant staying in our rather expensive home. And we accepted that that, in turn, meant one of us—the one making more money—had to work even longer hours. It seemed necessary to have a home that looked like a home, if we were ever to have children, which we kept feeling we would want next year. That's life, we both said, and shrugged. During the workday, we texted each other often.

These days, we have a good division of labor in the household. We hug each other often, to convey support. We cook—dinner, sometimes breakfast, and definitely brunch on weekends. We own a humidifier.

We're big on personal hygiene—a shower or a bath every day, sometimes two. Showers and baths are taken separately, for convenience. We fantasize about a big house. Our big house would have exposed-brick walls, a fireplace, and a

Jacuzzi where two people could bathe together and save time. The big house is not our only fantasy: sometimes we fantasize about other people. (*It's only natural*, we remind ourselves; we try to forget our past.) We eat cereal frequently. We often stay up late. We take turns buying soap and toilet paper. We never watch Doctor Phil.

Occasionally, we see our friends, many of whom have developed a drinking problem. They spike their iced teas, lean back and stare at things we can't see. They don't touch the tips of our shoulders. They ask about our house and our jobs, and we ask about theirs, but most of the time no one answers. Sometimes they ask about our old spouses, about how they're doing. We say we hear one of them got a dog, the other a cat. We say both of them have moved away. We say from all accounts they are happy, dating. For all we know, these things could be true.

Sometimes we go to parties. We talk to new people at these parties—some couples, some who are not coupled. These people are mostly attractive, and sometimes they say things like *Hi, I'm Shira.* They find an excuse to touch one of us while the other is eating Brie in another part of the room. *I love your shirt; is it silk?*

When we come home, we look for gray spots under our skin. We shake a little as we uncover ourselves to see. Every time, our skin is clear. We stand there for a moment, looking. Then we start touching each other with relief.

We realize, of course, that one day the force may strike again, leaving one of us breathless at the side of the road. We realize, but we try not to think about that. When we do, we say things like This understanding only makes us stronger. Sometimes one of us nods, says, *Right*, then adds, *But how, exactly?* It's as if all that exists for us is the present, the other says; in it, we must stand still, hold each other firmly.

THE THING ABOUT SOPHIA

Saturday

Saturdays we'd have brunch at Curly's. Sophia said Definitely Curly's, no brunch in the city better than Curly's and no neighborhood better than the East Village on a Saturday morning. She said morning but really she meant afternoon.

At Curly's they serve brunch till four p.m. on Saturdays. Anything you want done vegan you can get, and if you asked Sophia that's just the way the world should be. We always got too much food, but too much food on purpose is different from too much food by mistake; when there's no miscalculation involved, too much food is simply called supper, or sometimes brunch for Sunday. Also at Curly's, they give you a brunch drink for free with every brunch entrée ordered. Also tea. If you say you don't like tea and can you please get two drinks instead, sometimes they say yes, sometimes no. One of the things about Sophia: she asks questions, the world says yes. Two of the waitresses became her friends, a third fell in love. So Saturdays at Curly's, usually we got buzzed, and fake bacon never tasted better.

What happens when you get buzzed but you're already a little bit buzzed from the night before is that you feel *free.* So Saturdays at Curly's was the time of the week when I would say things to Sophia like I love you so much, you are the best roommate anyone could ask for, and the worst: I hope we'll be like this forever. Kir in hand, Sophia would laugh every time, finger my cheekbones (both sides, slowly), and say, Booney-Boo, you know there's no such thing as forever.

Sunday

Even though microwave-heated Curly's huevos rancheros is nothing like the original, brunching with Sophia on our living-room floor (we only got a coffee table two weeks before I moved out) was my favorite Sunday activity. I'd get the blue-yellow blanket from the bedroom and we'd call it Indoor Picnic.

But not every Sunday was Indoor Picnic Sunday. Some Sundays Sophia would wake up in the morning and, after brushing her teeth and before getting coffee, say, I can't be domesticated today. I knew better than to show disappointment, because show Sophia that you're disappointed and you can count on being alone for a week. So I'd say, Cool, what'd you have in mind?, because that was my way of saying maybe we can do something undomesticated together. But when Sophia wanted to feel undomesticated it usually meant she needed time away from me, so she'd say, Oh, you know I can't think before my first cup of coffee.

A good time to explain about the bedroom: when I first moved in, the two rooms were both called bedrooms, and the rest of the apartment was a space we shared. Then one Sunday morning Sophia said, Let's make the small room a recording studio. Sophia was buying another guitar then and all kinds of expensive equipment, and I was mostly sleeping in her room anyway, so it seemed sensible. She said, If I have a studio I'll have to get serious. I thought she was already plenty serious about her music, but Sophia was always looking for ways to get serious about things, and if you said anything back that sounded like advice, all of a sudden you were her enemy. Then you needed to make it up to her, and that wasn't always easy, so the best way was to say, That's a great idea. I said, That's a great idea, and that's how Sophia's bedroom became our bedroom and my room became her studio.

Another thing that sometimes happened on Sundays was End of Weekend Blues. That was especially common on Indoor Picnic Sundays: when Sophia looked outside and the window said evening, she would get antsy, like she was waiting for someone to arrive. I had to be careful, because when she got like that saying the wrong thing was something that could creep up on you. One minute there would be peacefulness, the next you were fighting with Sophia and you felt like she *hated* you, because Sophia doesn't know how to fight with the future in mind. Sophia fights like Sophia cooks like Sophia makes love like Sophia plays the guitar: as though possibly it's the last thing she'll ever do. Her eyes get so red there is no green left in them. Her lips get tight and lose their heart shape completely. She screams without stopping for air, and even if it's a day before a show, she forgets she is supposed to watch her voice. I know the reason: this is also a show, and it is no less important to her than any other. But when someone is throwing loud, hurtful words at you, your heart doesn't care about reasons. Sometimes she throws things, too.

Monday

Monday was Sophia's Errands Day. Sophia's definition for errands is Anything you hate to do, and her theory is it should all be compressed to one day or you end up believing your life sucks. So, for example, grocery shopping is not an errand, but calling her aunt Zelda is. If Sophia has a toothache and the receptionist says Thursday one week from today, Sophia will say Give me the next available Monday, because going to the dentist is an errand, and errands are done on Mondays. And if you tell her it doesn't make sense to suffer tooth pain longer than you have to, she'll make a face like she just swallowed something sour and say, Clearly, you don't know much about artists.

It was a Monday before Sophia meant anything to me, five, maybe six p.m., and I was standing at the door with my suitcases and everything. A while later, when I learned about Sophia's week, I realized I must have been one of her errands that Monday. *Interview Lydia's cousin.* The thing about Sophia, she opens the door, you see right away how beautiful she is; you see right away it's the kind of beauty everyone wants to share. I was funny to her then—first thing she did was laugh. I laughed too, because her laughter made me happy, even though I knew it was directed at me and didn't know why, which is usually unpleasant. Finally she said, Lydia couldn't have been more right. Lydia is a relative of mine, second-cousin-once-removed sort of relative, and she was the one to say, You go ahead and move to the city and you'll see things will just work out. She gave me Sophia's number, and on the phone Sophia gave me the address and said, See you then, so I assumed I was moving in. I didn't know then that in New York people interview other people to be roommates; I thought you usually went on interviews when you wanted other people to hire you, pay you, not when you wanted to pay them. I packed everything I had—which wasn't much, because the man I was leaving was the kind who sues if you take stuff—in two suitcases and one huge handbag. I took a cab from Penn Station and told myself the stuff was simply too heavy, but really I was just afraid of the subway. Then: Sophia, laughing, and I knew right away, though it still took some time to figure out.

Tuesday

Tuesdays Sophia usually spent the day auditioning people for her band. If she liked someone (usually a drummer), that person would be auditioning other people with her the following Tuesday, but often by the Tuesday after that they'd be gone; it rarely took Sophia more than a week to discover Disparities in Artistic Visions.

Sophia loved those Tuesdays, and the more people showed up, the happier she was. Really, when you think about it, Sophia was auditioning all the time, not just on Tuesdays; some auditions were simply more official than others. Sophia ran auditions for friends, for lovers, for people who might cook for her or tell her things she didn't know. And people just kept showing up, trying their hardest, because that's the thing about Sophia: she makes you feel like her approval is the one ingredient you're missing.

Let me explain about the finances, though my knowledge is limited. I shared a bed with Sophia for over a year, and in that year more often than not we appeared to the world as two halves of a thing, but still: what Sophia doesn't want to discuss she won't, and good luck to you if you think What's the harm in just raising the question. So here's what I do know: Sophia doesn't have to work. There is no lavishness about her, but she firmly believes that needs should be met. If a certain need means money, then money will be spent; but mostly Sophia thinks about money the way most people think of socks—sometimes essential, at other times unnecessary, but either way not an interesting topic for conversation or thought.

Over time I've heard more than one theory about Sophia's finances, because people think if someone who has money isn't interested in money there must be something they don't know, and when people think there's something they don't know, they talk. Lydia said a trust fund, and Lydia has known Sophia for years, so possibly that's right. In fact, that was one of the first things she told me when we talked about my leaving that jerk and moving to New York. She said A friend of mine, said We go way back, and said She's living off a trust fund that would last her great-grandkids if she ever has any, and she's pretty generous, so maybe you won't have to worry about money for a while.

Of course I always worry about money, and living with Sophia didn't change that at all.

One night at a party we were throwing, a very tall girl who seemed to know a lot about Sophia said, Babe, I'd be dreading Monday so bad if it weren't for you, and touched Sophia's arm, and Sophia smiled and went to the kitchen to get more beer. What's Monday? I asked the tall girl, because that was before I learned that Sophia's people often judged you by how much you really knew about Sophia. The tall girl snorted and said, The shoot; once a year she still has to do it or there'll be no money for pretty girls like you to live off her. I don't live off her, I said all deadpan, and got up to go help Sophia with the beer; but really I felt happy that she said I was pretty. So that was the second theory I heard.

Then, once, Sophia said, An old friend will be staying with us a couple of nights, and when the old friend arrived she was young and beautiful and Sophia's ex. Her name was Anna but Sophia called her Honeydew. Sophia rarely called anyone by their given name. For a whole evening it was Honeydew remember this and Honeydew remember that, and Of course, Sophie, how could I ever forget. I felt unnecessary, but we were drinking a lot and gradually it got better. At some point I looked out the window, and even though I squinted I still couldn't tell if it was dark or bright, and I couldn't remember in which room we kept the clock, and I heard Anna giggle and say, Is he still sending you *that* much every month? and You should really see that stock person I told you about, Sophie, you're being irresponsible. So that was the third theory I heard about Sophia's money, except I had no idea what I heard.

Wednesday

On Wednesdays, Sophia was a volunteer. Every few weeks she would choose a new organization, because the thing about Sophia is, she gets bored easily. One sure way to make Sophia smile is find a not-for-profit she hasn't heard of, because what happens when you volunteer Sophia-style is that you run out of causes.

Here's why I said if Sophia doesn't want to discuss something she won't: the day Anna left was a Wednesday, and I woke Sophia up two hours after we'd gone to bed because she was supposed to be at Cooper Union, selling tickets for a PEN festival event. Sophia said, I'm not going. I looked at her and didn't know what to say; Sophia was usually very strict about her weekly routine. She said, I'm totally hungover, I need to rest, and the PEN people will be fine without me; it's not a shelter for homeless children with AIDS, you know, so don't look at me like that. She must have read my surprise as criticism, which couldn't have been further from the truth; the rigidity of her schedule always made me feel superfluous somehow, and now I was thinking maybe change is possible, maybe from now on Wednesdays will be something new, maybe Anna's visit is actually a story with a happy ending. I called in sick to the gallery—which I had never done before, because I believed excelling at that job was my best shot at becoming a real New Yorker—and said to Sophia, Maybe we can spend the morning together. I put all the stuff in the blender to make our special hangover juice, and she made a face but drank it all, which made me hopeful, as if this somehow meant I was wrong to be worried about Anna. In a moment I will ask Sophia, and she'll laugh and say, Anna? Really? Oh, Booney-Boo, you're sweet when you're insecure, and our happy ending will begin.

The thing about Sophia, you can't show her jealousy or

she'll remember why she hates commitment and explain it to you until you lock yourself in the bathroom to make her stop. The truth is, in any relationship someone at some point is locked in a bathroom. It isn't the end of the world. But it is better to be smart, and with Sophia a way to be smart is, when you ask about other people, pretend you're asking something else. Say, Anna reminds me of someone but I can't figure out who, or, How come Anna isn't over more often? You two seem really good friends. For it to work, Sophia needs to pretend right along with you, though, and that Wednesday the hangover made her too tired for acting; I shouldn't have brought it up just then, but there was something like an itch in my neck where I feel urgency, and it was not the kind that would go away if I went to the gallery and tried to focus on work.

Sophia said, Boon, I love a lot of people, I share my life with a lot of people, I told you this the very first night. She was being honest, and it scared me, but you don't start a talk like that and then change your mind. I said, This is different, though, with Anna, right? I spoke very quietly but it still sounded loud in my head. And childish. Sophia said, Anna is from another life, another time. I nodded. We have a history together, she said, the kind that makes you dependent. Sophia didn't usually say things like that. She seemed exhausted, and for a minute I thought maybe we were together inside her dream. Then she closed her eyes, and I knew that when she woke up she would wonder, at least for a moment, if this conversation truly happened.

Thursday

Thursday mornings Sophia and I went grocery shopping, and on the Thursdays when we hosted a party at night, grocery shopping was a thing that took its time. When Sophia first got me the job at the gallery, she said, But you can never work Thursday mornings—that's when we get food for the week. She was talking to me as a roommate; I'd just moved in. I said But maybe if I work the morning shift we can go in the afternoon, and she said, Tell them you can never work mornings on Thursdays, and don't say why; it will only make them appreciate you.

Thursday was Sophia's favorite Party Night, and we usually went out dancing or invited a bunch of people over, who brought music and amplifiers and drugs and called Sophia Gorgeous and Goddess and Sophia Loren. *Hey, Sophia Loren, awesome party.* At these parties, people often had sex at different locations in our apartment, using things like kitchen supplies as props.

A good time to talk about the sex: we had a lot of it, except at the end, and it was always good, except when it wasn't. This is when it wasn't good: on Thursdays, when other people were in on it, and especially when Sophia assumed I had my own interests for the night. I did not, because that's the thing about Sophia: she gives you the kind of freedom you don't want.

Before I met Sophia, I never thought of myself as a woman who could be with women this way, and maybe I'm not, maybe it's only with Sophia. But my sense is, it's the kind of thing that once you let it in, it is going to play itself out.

When I called Lydia to let her know I was all settled in, as we'd agreed I'd do, she said, Well, has she fucked you yet, and I said, What do you mean, you said she's a nice and generous person. As I said before, I knew but I did not yet want to know. Lydia said, I'm talking about sex—have you had sex yet, and she sounded tired like I was an assignment she had to complete. I said, No . . . I'm not gay, Lydia, and Lydia said, Right, right. Then she said, Do you know what a rollercoaster is? And I knew she didn't mean the regular kind so I said no and she said, Why don't you ask Sophia about that.

I did. I asked Sophia, and she laughed her Lydia laughter, like that first day in the hallway: head tilted all the way back like she was trying to reach the floor, and something liberating like relief emanating from her lungs. We touched each other for the first time that night until the outside looked purple and small butterflies were flapping their wings against some inner wall I never knew I had. We lay in bed after, me facing the window, where Sophia had the strangest-looking plant; its leaves had a redness to them that made the whole thing look plastic, and I had the urge to touch it and see whether or not it was real, but I couldn't reach it. I sat up, wings still fluttering in me, and said to Sophia, I'm not a lesbian, though, and Sophia smiled a new smile and said, Sweet Booney.

Friday

For the first few months, every Friday was City Lessons Day. Before I moved in, Friday was something else, but I never found out what. So Fridays we would take out a map of Manhattan, a subway map, and sometimes maps of other boroughs too. I also had a blue spiral notebook for tips that seemed important. Sophia started this tradition because, one day in the Village, walking east, I asked how much farther we had to walk to hit Central Park. She looked at me then like maybe I'd just turned out to be a mistake. This look had a sting and I thought, when someone looks at you this way you'll never get to go with them to their dark places, and all I ever wanted, since that first moment in the hallway, was to be the person Sophia reached for when she cried. I said, I don't even know how long I'll live here, so I just don't bother with the city. Sophia nodded, and I knew I'd said the right thing. I was just starting to learn then how to be a woman who intrigued her. Then she said, But will you let me teach you, Boon? I mean, you do live here for now. I said Maybe. She liked that answer. Then, the following Friday: the maps, the spiral notebook, and Sophia saying, Tip number one, in New York City, if you reach Chinatown you've gone too far.

Saturday

Saturdays we'd have brunch at Curly's, and, more than any other place and more than any other time, I felt envied at Curly's, because I was Sophia's Saturday-morning person, and everyone knows that's something you can't beat.

Once, the waitress was rude to me—the same waitress who was always asking Sophia out. Being rude by way of hitting on the woman you're with when you're peeing is different from being rude to your face, from saying, No you *didn't* say provolone, I'd remember. Sophia said, If you don't like it here anymore we'll find somewhere else, Boon, and I knew then that something was different.

Saturdays at Curly's we put salt on our curly fries like powder. Every time Sophia would say, It's not good, we're dehydrated as it is, but she said it like you say *I know, I know* when a friend says something true you don't want to hear. Because Saturdays at Curly's we didn't want to hear that salt is bad for you, that alcohol dries you up, that other women can come on to your woman when you're looking away, that in love sometimes you blink and when you open your eyes there's change.

Saturdays at Curly's it was warm, then cold and then snowing, and always people were waiting outside or by the radiator, and always we didn't have to wait, because the thing about Sophia is, she doesn't like to wait in lines, and mostly the world agrees she shouldn't have to.

Saturdays at Curly's we always stayed for hours—long after we were too full, long after we stopped feeling the pain of stretch in our stomachs—and played checkers or drew on white paper mats with crayons. Saturdays at Curly's I would look at the people crouched over the radiator, being pushed against the small door every time someone entered to add her name to the list, to ask about the wait. Saturdays at Curly's I felt privileged, and guilty, and sometimes I would look at Sophia and see that she felt neither.

Saturdays at Curly's, looking at the people outside, sometimes this is what I wanted: to be one of them. Saturdays at Curly's, when Sophia was suddenly flexible about where we brunched, she looked like she was trying on a new dress that didn't fit her, and it made me sad, like reaching the end of a good novel. The thing about Sophia is, you love someone like her, it's for good, it becomes part of your body, an organ. But Saturdays at Curly's sometimes I would think, maybe I can take this organ and leave, go to a place where I can wait with the rest of the world by the radiator, feeling the chill of icy wind every time the door opens, because maybe that's what life is about: waiting your turn.

NONE THE WISER

I'm sure they have things in common, yes. But not a whole lot. Not a whole lot. I'm sure they have things in common, Ludvig and Henrietta, but I'm not sure what these things might be. To be quite honest, if someone asked me to guess—just venture a guess as to what these two people could possibly have in common, what it is that got them to suddenly "fall in love" at such a late point in life—I would have to say, "I'm sorry, but I have absolutely no idea." And then maybe the person would say, "Of course you have no idea, that's why they call it *a guess*" and I would say, "I'm truly sorry, sir"—or madam; perhaps it would be a woman saying these things to me—"but I couldn't even *guess*." It brings to mind that expression "to save my life"; as in "I couldn't guess to save my life." That's how I feel about them. Or not about them, really, just about their relationship; they are very nice people, kind people, both of them. Especially him.

He used to collect seashells. Years ago, I am talking about years ago. Back when they were both married to other people and didn't even know each other, back when my Saul was alive, that's when Ludvig collected those seashells. He would show me, every time we had one of our gatherings. Look at this special one, Yolanda, he'd always say, and always away from the gang, waiting for me outside the kitchen or by the big window in the hallway. Look at this special one. I used to wonder back then if he ever showed them to his Judith, and I had a feeling he didn't. Certain things you only share with certain people—nothing wrong with that. And why me, I also wondered sometimes. Because he knew I understood, was my answer. And I really did, I understood. It's only a man with a soul who does something like that—collect seashells. And what a rare thing that is, a man with a soul.

And Henrietta? Once, years ago, at one of the big parties we threw—I am fairly certain Ludvig wasn't there, because I tried to think back after they got together and I don't think they ever crossed paths, not in those years at least, and not through us—my husband announced to all our guests that he was going to get rid of his pipe, quit smoking. He was drunk. It's both the best and worst of us that comes out when we drink, isn't it? He didn't want to quit; he wanted to *have quit.* And I think everyone understood that, saw the moment for what it was—an inebriated man saying Oh how I wish life was something else, something better. But she is not everyone; she is a special woman. Very special. At the end of the night, she handed me seven pipes. I didn't know my husband had so many. "He's going to need all the help he can get," she said. Apparently, her uncle had died of throat cancer. Or it might have been her brother. I didn't know her well at all then—I don't think Saul Keningstein and my Saul were even in business yet, I think they had only just met, and we invited him and his wife to the party. So I was a little surprised. "The first step to beating addiction is removing the abused substance from the household," she said. It was a caring gesture, I suppose. Of course she did sound a bit like she'd memorized a brochure. Who in their right mind would memorize a brochure? I've certainly never felt inspired to memorize a brochure, and Lord knows I've seen my share of them in my seventy-nine years. And one *could* argue, I suppose, that she shouldn't have gone through our belongings looking for pipes; no one asked her to do that. I certainly didn't ask her, and I was the only one who could, because it was my house. Mine and my Saul's, of course, but why would he ask her to look for the pipes? He knew where they were, he was the one who put them wherever she found them. And he didn't want them gone. It would have been quite a perverted little game for the two of them to play. And my husband was never like that. There were times when I wished he'd be a little more like that, in fact. *Playful.* But it wasn't his nature. A man's nature is not something you can change. Women who think otherwise end up divorced.

So my husband certainly didn't ask her to do it, and I didn't ask her to do it, and so, yes, you could say, I suppose, that it was presumptuous of her. Nosy. Ill intended. But

I didn't think that at all. I appreciated it, and I thought: What a caring gesture. I thought: Isn't Saul Keningstein lucky, to have such a *lovely* woman for a wife. Truly.

It was towels, when they first got started, Saul Keningstein and my Saul. To be honest, I thought it was nonsense. I never liked Saul Keningstein much—he was a hustler, if you ask me. Every time he opened his mouth it was Let me tell you something. *Let me tell you something, Yolanda dear.* And I always wanted to say Maybe every once in a while you should ask a question, Saul Keningstein. But he knew everything, so why should he ask? I remember I said to my Saul, I said This is nonsense. You are a doctor. What do you need to be selling towels for? But these were special towels, soft and airy like clouds in the sky, something America had never seen. I said Saul, you have been here your whole life almost and still you think like an immigrant. He was always trying to prove that he had the right to be here, that America made the right decision letting his family in when he was seven years old. What can you do? Being a doctor wasn't enough. He had to do something *new*, a first in America. Even if it was a towel. So I said, Fine, fine. Just be careful, don't invest too much. But I didn't worry; he was responsible, my Saul. So responsible. And what did I know, anyway? Saul Keningstein was right, the towels did very well.

When I say that for the life of me I couldn't guess what Ludvig and Henrietta have in common, please understand—I am not saying anything about them as people. I have absolutely nothing against them. They are both lovely. I'm making a statement about their relationship, is how you could put it. Although, well, that's not right either. What do I know about their relationship? Only what I see. And they seem happy, I suppose, when one looks at them. The issue has to do with *compatibility.* I think the young generation pays little attention to the concept of compatibility. And that isn't to say that they are young, Ludvig and Henrietta. They are not young. Ludvig went to medical school with my Saul, which means he's more or less as old as I am. That is not young. I do not enjoy discussing it, but it is the truth. I refuse to be one of those old ladies who holds a shaking spoon over her soup and says "I am not old" or "I feel young." Feelings don't matter, behaviors do. People who don't understand this simple fact are unemployed or incarcerated.

In plain English, it is a lie; when you hold a spoon over a bowl of soup and your hand is shaking, you do not feel young. You feel old. So I am old, and Ludvig is old, too. Henrietta is a little younger, but that doesn't make her young. She is old. Henrietta might think she's young. Her grandchildren come to visit and she tells them stories about the things she used to do when she was younger, but it is all one big exaggeration—she did not "run the union," and people never "quivered at the sight of her"; she just answered the phone. Or she might have done a little more than answering the phone, and her boss certainly liked her—I will not go into the rumors about her and Mr. Burt, whether or not it was truly for him that she left Saul Keningstein and their children; perhaps it was only coincidence that they both disappeared at the same time—but that does not mean that she "ran the union." She did not run the union. That is preposterous.

And who does something like that, anyway, leave? I don't mean to be judgmental—Saul always used to say, Don't be so judgmental, Yoli—but I never could understand it, to be honest. Leaving a man is one thing, though back then it was quite unheard of. But a mother leaving her own children for a whole year? I am not a judgmental woman, but that's quite something. And when she came back, it was only to take the children away. Poor Saul Keningstein. He had his money and his ladies, but he was a different man after that, a pale man. If you marry a man, you're not supposed to do anything that would change the color of his skin. That much I know. I never left Saul—forty-two years we were together, and not all of them easy. Don't get me wrong—we were the best of friends, but forty-two years is a lifetime, and in any lifetime there's hardship. But leaving? Never crossed my mind. And if we had children, well, I can only imagine. No doubt leaving would have been even further from my mind.

So Henrietta is a bit younger, yes, but she is old; they are both old. And people who are old should be wise, because if not that, what is the point? Nothing works like it used to. The body, I mean—it does not operate as it once did. Everything takes a long time—you want to make an omelet, you'd better have a couple of free hours. And the people who used to ask you about your day—*How was your day, my sweet Yoli?*—and the people you used to invite over when you threw parties, and the people who'd pick up the phone to call you when the Laundromat lost their favorite jacket—they're all gone. So if you don't have some wisdom to show, then I honestly don't understand what the point of it all might be.

I don't mean to sound suicidal. I am not suicidal. And I certainly do have my wisdom, thank God, even though that's not a thing one is supposed to say about oneself. But it is true nonetheless; I am a wise woman, and when I have to go to the bathroom four minutes after I went to the bathroom the last time—at least I can tell myself, Yolanda, you are a wise woman, and you are wiser today than ever before thanks to all the years you've been on this earth. You know that expression "none the wiser"? That does not apply to me.

Part of being wise when you are old is detecting what stupidity younger people are up to, and making sure to avoid it. This isn't hard to do. And yet so many old people embrace the stupidities of the younger generation because they think this will make them younger. How silly. Nothing makes you younger, nothing at all. But that is what they think—they will behave like their grandchildren and use the funny words that they are using and learn how to operate the computer and they will be younger, or appear younger, which they believe is the same. It is not the same.

What I'm trying to say is that younger people nowadays pay no attention to this important thing called *compatibility*, and that Ludvig and Henrietta, because they are the kind of people who are always trying to be younger, are doing the same thing. How else would you explain this haste? Judith was gone, and whoosh, right away, a new couple was born, Ludvig and Henrietta. I don't mean to criticize him—Ludvig took care of Judith for many years. She was never a healthy woman, always some issue, even when we were all young. And the last few years—better not to think about it. I always knew he was a special one, but the way he took care of her—that was something you don't see every day. But what does his dedication have to do with Henrietta, with being compatible or not? Nothing. When you move so fast, you don't have time to think, look into things, other possibilities. Because for example, there might be plenty of women more suitable for Ludvig. Women who adore seashells. Women who don't abandon men. That is all I'm trying to say. These women might be out there, waiting for him.

When you walk on the beach in the early-morning hours, your eyes are scouting the sand and your feet are waiting for the smoothness of that tiny piece of marble. When you stop to pick one up, the wind slows down. I am not a sentimental woman; this is a fact—the wind slows down. My years on this earth have taught me to notice the small ways in which people and nature collaborate. The wind slows down, and while you are almost eighty years old, you are also a newborn. This is a fact. You put the seashell to your ear, this telephone of the ocean. You listen to the sound of something both beyond and within your reach. And you hope. Because after a certain point, what's between you and a casket except hope? So you hope.

What a silly invitation it was that I got from Henrietta. Some nonsense about an organization that sends knitted socks to children with bare feet in cold climates. She was apparently volunteering there now, and was hosting an event for them. Nonsense. I knew right away something was up—Henrietta never threw parties. And this whole sock business didn't sound right. But I didn't think it had anything to do with Ludvig—why would I? I didn't even know they'd met. And for all I knew he was in mourning. I had reached out, of course, after I heard of Judith's passing. I said Anything you need, Ludvig, you just let me know, anything at all.

I was thinking I would give him some time and then call again. He deserves all the support he can get, I thought. And he was always a good friend to my Saul, referring patients any chance he got. I imagined he'd be the kind of widower who'd hide in a dark room for a long time, perhaps until a woman came and showed him how to be outside again, taught him that you still breathe after something like that—just a little different, a little lower is all.

When the body doesn't want you breathing deep anymore, you don't argue. People who don't understand this end up dead before their time. What you do is you say Thank you for the oxygen, and you breathe low. This is something I learned after Saul, and I was thinking on the phone with Ludvig I should teach him, because I could hear his effort. But I didn't, I just said Anything you need, Ludvig, you let me know, because I thought, Yolanda, give him time. People need time to grieve their grief the wrong way first. Who would have thought he'd need so little of it?

A new relationship is nobody's business, if you ask me. It needs the attention of the people who are in it, not the people around it. And one thing I have learned is when you look at other people looking at you, you end up seeing the wrong things. Young people today, they have it all wrong. They think you have to show your happiness all the time. And there they were, Ludvig and Henrietta, silly like young people, announcing their love to everyone. Not with words, of course, but you live as long as I have, you know words matter very little. Especially words like *volunteer* or *orphans*—those are words people say only when they mean something else. Henrietta and Ludvig were announcing their new love with their hands—they were holding hands. They were greeting everyone at the door, Ludvig in a suit and a bow tie—I had never seen him wear a bow tie—and they were holding hands.

I thought for a moment this must be some sort of mistake—how do they even know each other? And what would they possibly have in common? They are such different people. But of course it wasn't a mistake.

Henrietta said Yolanda, would you consider joining us? I think you'd find it *so gratifying.* Gratifying, she said—I would find socks gratifying. I said I'm sure I would, but you know in all honesty since Saul I don't get out of the house much. I looked at Ludvig when I said it, to make sure he heard. And of course Henrietta said Oh that's not good Yolanda and all that nonsense—she's a lovely woman, but if there's any way to use a slogan you can be sure Henrietta will do it. She quoted something about grief—I can't remember what and I didn't quite listen, because I wanted to say What do you know about grief, Henrietta? You can't abandon your husband and then teach other people about grief. But her abandoning, that was many years ago. No one cares about that anymore, I suppose. No one cares that not all grief is the same. So I said You're right, Henrietta, you're absolutely right. I looked at Ludvig again when I said it. He nodded. Henrietta always liked to hear she was right.

THAT NIGHT

1.

We have been indoors for many days and long nights now, due to fear of disappointment. Our fear is rational, fact-based. When we go outside—if we go outside—we will be devastated. We will want life to feel as it did that night, and life will fail us. After that night at Lamplight with Gary, life is bound to forever fail us.

2.

That night, we spoke with abandon. We drank in good rhythm. We befriended former lovers, tapped their left shoulder with only one finger, even though we were many. Do you go to the gym, we asked each other that night. Do you at least *plan* to go? But we never answered. We didn't have to.

That night, we counted uncountable things—the advantages of dairy, the siblings we never had. There were moments when we twirled our hair coyly, and in those moments our hair was the kind that twirls well. When we hummed, everyone enjoyed it. Our smiles were the texture of ice cream, which is to say we could be cold and still perceived as sweet. It was our birthday that night, it was Gary's book party, it was everyone's Christmas. We didn't know it walking in, but it was true, and we had the gifts to prove it. The more we gifted, the more we got, and Lamplight was getting wrapping-paper crowded. Isn't there an old adage about that, someone asked. And there was. There was an old adage.

3.

We had no special expectations that night—just Gary, reading. He had never been a poet before, or if he was, we knew nothing of it. He was a foot surgeon last we saw him, which was in Argentina and a while back. Before that he sold snakes to collectors, and before that the cooking show, of course—the one that made him famous.

———

You can't see Gary and *not* want to bed him, but that night wasn't about sex. Walking into Lamplight and seeing Gary, we knew that right away. Tonight was too good for sex.

4.

We danced ourselves happy that night, lightness in our toes, our heels. But we were also productive, successful. We found solutions to problems, fixed things that were previously broken. Some people were cooking or baking, some were inventing gadgets that would replace umbrellas. It wasn't raining that night, not yet, but we were seeing the bigger picture. Everyone felt understood. It was an unspoken rule that night—if anyone said anything, everyone stopped and listened. We followed with nodding, just to make sure.

5.

When we stepped outside, it was pouring but silent. We stood there, looking at the rain, hearing nothing. Strange, isn't it, we said half to Gary, half to the sky. Some storms are silent, Gary said, shrugging. In his head, he was already under the covers, perhaps with a lady or two. Sometimes Gary was a tourist, but that night he was savvy. He knew the ways of our town. Come home with us, we whispered. We wanted to touch his cheek, but we knew better. This wasn't Argentina. I had a good time, Gary said. Thanks. He smiled his Gary smile at us, and we knew the night was over.

6.

Indoors, the walls are inching toward us. Every few hours, we measure the distance. The rain is loud outside, always loud, and we try not to listen. We talk about that night a lot, but as time goes by, it gets harder to remember. Did we grow strawberries? we ask. Did we suck on their long stems, did it make Gary laugh? We usually say yes, yes we did. Gary laughed, we say, he laughed his quiet Gary laugh. But we can never be sure.

Every once in a while, the rain seems to stop. We look out the window, and it's hard to tell; all we see is wetness and fog. But it doesn't matter. What matters is the loudness quiets down. We gather in the center of the room so we won't measure the distance. We sit in a circle and try to pretend that we are back at Lamplight. We sit in a circle and listen to the silence until we remember loud enough to feel.

FULLY ZIPPED

1.

As I enter the fitting room, the woman says, My name is Andy, if you need anything.

What is your name if I don't need anything? I ask.

2.

As I enter the fitting room, the woman asks, What's your name?

Dora Freud, I say.

Have I pushed it too far? Probably not. In the fitting-room world, I've learned, too far doesn't happen easy.

She doesn't blink. Dora, my name is Lauren if you need anything.

3.

As I enter the fitting room, the woman counts the clothes I have picked. Using blue chalk, she writes a number on the fitting-room door. Seven.

She is wrong. I have eight items. Briefly, I stare at the woman's mistake. I say nothing, and by saying nothing I transform the mistake into a lie.

4.

As I enter the fitting room, the woman counts the clothes I have picked, and as she is counting she is avoiding my eyes. She is looking at the line behind me. What is your name, I want to ask her, and Don't you want to know mine? But this is not that kind of place.

I try on a blue dress that ties at the back. I can't ask the woman for help because she didn't offer it, and because as a rule I try to avoid the words "excuse me." I especially try to avoid the words "excuse me" when the next words are "can you zip me up?"

Instead, I look in the mirror with my eyes closed. I'm trying to picture what the blue dress would look like fully zipped.

5.

As I enter the fitting room, the woman says, Let me know if you need any sizes.

You're not that hot either, I tell her.

6.

As I enter the fitting room, the woman asks me how I am today. How are you today, she says. It sounds like the beginning of a song. Not so great, I tell her; my dog just died. Brownie. I've had him since I was eight. Oh, she says. My dog sitter killed him, I add. She seems confused and I don't know how to help her. Well, she says, let me know if you need anything.

7.

As I enter the fitting room, the woman says, Here, try this, too. She is handing me a navy-blue blazer. This is a small store, the kind some people call "boutique." There is no one around but us. Is this your store? I ask. I like knowing what's at stake. The blazer hangs between us on her outstretched arm as I wait for her answer. She shakes her head no, says, My aunt's. She's probably lying. I look around to be sure. No one's aunt owns this store. Just thought you might like it, she says, I have the same one. She starts to turn around, but I grab the blazer first, to be polite. She did pick it just for me.

When I'm alone in the room, I look at the blazer, touch the inside of its only pocket with one finger. Maybe the woman wasn't lying after all. I think about what it means—what it could mean—for two women to pick each other's clothes. I want to know her closet as well as I know my own. I want to show her mine. I want us to coparent clothing items.

The blazer doesn't fit. It makes me look like a man. I step outside anyway. Wow, the woman says, wow. I shake my head no. She seems shocked. You can't be serious, she says. How do I explain that I wanted to love it? How do I explain that choosing something to wear means rejecting all the other clothes in the world, all the other selves I could be? I want to ask if she would like to have coffee one morning; in the mornings I explain myself much better. Thank you for your time, I say. Come back another day, she says. I smile, and the woman smiles back. Whether she lied earlier about the store or not, right now I can tell she's telling the truth.

8.

As I enter the fitting room, I close the door and stand in my underwear in front of the mirror, afraid. I want to feel that my life cannot go on without this dress. It's a beige dress with a white collar. There are tiny white butterflies all over, but you need to look closely to see. I slow down, slow down, slow down. But I can't slow down enough. The moment still comes when I try it on and don't fall in love. Falling in love never comes easy to me. I look at my disappointment. I say to my disappointment, Let's keep trying. There is no intention in me when I say it, no truth. But I say it again, because even the worst lie turns real if you repeat it enough. Let's keep trying.

9.

As I enter the fitting room, I regret avoiding the woman; I feel ready for eye contact. I stop and look, wait until she looks back. Hi, I say. Hi, she says, and starts moving toward me; can I help you? You helped me the other day, I say, with the blazer? I remember you, she says, and I nod because I'm not sure what to say. Are you going to try anything on? she asks. I am not holding any clothes. I've been thinking about that blazer, I tell her, that maybe it was just a new look, something I wasn't used to. Can I see it again? I'm so sorry, she says, we sold that one. Her eyebrows are apologizing too. It's gone.

10.

As I enter the fitting room, I wait for the knock on the door, followed by the saleswoman's voice. How are you doing in there? she asks. You need anything?

WE, THE WOMEN

We, the people of the great American city, we leave our city twice every week, and head north. Up north, there is a small American town where we, the people of the great American city, can learn new things.

There, in the small American town, we perfect our craft. We seek inspiration. We become a community. There, in the small American town, we are assigned mentors, and those mentors tell us that they once used to be just like us, young people of the great American city, traveling north in search of knowledge.

We, the people of the great American city, we are, in fact, women. Up north, we learn our gender is important. We sit on green velvet rugs and stare at dark wood burning in the fireplace, our mentors saying, *Look beyond; imagine.* Up north, we learn that fire is a screen, we learn to dream. Our mentors, they tell us of a world where women scratch tomatoes with their nails and the fruit doesn't bleed. Up north, we think maybe that world can one day be our world.

We, the women of the great American city, when we are not up north, we roam our urban streets. We look for inspiration to hide inside our purses, we look for the kind that travels well. Instead, we, the women of the great American city, we find men. These men, they are not the men we have at home, waiting for us with a cooked meal. These men, they try to buy us and we try to ignore them, because up north, in the small American town, we've been taught that *no* comes in many forms.

We, the women of the great American city, we turn our backs on these men, and they then grade our backs, grade our asses. We, the women of the great American city, we usually get a ten. This ten, it excites us and revolts us, and we throw up at the side of the road. We, the women of the great American city, we then go home to our meal-cooking men, and our men see the remnants of puke on our lips and know what the streets of the big American city were like today. Our men, they wipe our faces clean of puke, and kiss our chaste, voluptuous lips.

We, the women of the great American city, we fuck our men on hot summer nights, because we despise weakness, and fucking feels like strength. We fuck our men whether we feel like it or not; we climb on top of them to prove a point, and the scent of our intestines has yet to fade.

We, the women of the great American city, we row the muscles of our men until they cannot tell pleasure from pain. Then we row some more. (We, the women of the great American city, we use our bodies to speak our minds.) We enjoy inflicting pain upon our men, and when they cry, we lick their tears: returning the favor of compassion.

We, the women of the great American city, we slap our men's cheeks when they are dry of tears—we slap them hard. Our men, some of them don't understand, and we, the women of the great American city, we have to explain it to them.

This is how we explain: we hold our men by their balls, and we squeeze. This squeeze, it hurts them, but it is necessary. This squeeze, it explains to them by way of the body, by way of pain, that we know. We know, the unbearable pain in their crotch tells them in no uncertain terms, that they, too, were once ass-grading men on the streets of the great American city. We know that deep down they still are, and further deep is where they always will be. Our men, they then cry like babies. Our men, they swear to us that they are different, that they love us.

We, the women of the great American city, the following morning we always drive north. We, the women of the great American city, we want to consult our mentors. This is what we want to know: how to trust. Our mentors, they say trust is overrated. They say the secret is simply *to be*, to get up in the morning without murder in your heart, and pour green tea into porcelain cups.

Every time we head back south we ask, *Have we learned enough?* Every time, we think, *Tonight, we will look the grading men straight in the eyes and say, Zero; your grade is zero. Tonight, we will not puke.* We, the women of the great American city, as we descend upon our city through the windows of our cars, our trains, our planes, as we descend upon our city, we try to pretend that on this journey we have educated ourselves about *trust*, about *puke.* We, the women of the great American city, we look at the great American city drawing to a close, and we know: at times there is murder in our hearts.

THE BEGINNING OF A PLAN

1991, Part I: My Escape

In 1991, I went to jail for canning goods without a license. My factory was small, really a mom-and-pop shop, but when they caught me it made national news, because they blamed the whole bruchtussis epidemic on me. A reporter named Dolly P. investigated my operation with the kind of zeal people mostly demonstrate when their children's lives are at risk. Dolly P. had no children, but she had ambition. She traced the first case to the same small town in Israel that manufactured most of my ingredients. For a while, every time a kid ate bad canned soup, it was my fault; the mother would go on television and cry, My baby is coughing all the time now, my baby never used to cough, and the newswoman would wipe away a tear, sigh, and remind the public once again that my trial would soon begin. I got ten years.

I was a tough woman, a strong woman. But even the

toughest human being feels the sting of mortality when the law comes and says, Give us the best decade of your life. I'd just turned twenty-one; it hadn't even been a year since I'd left Israel. I had to escape.

Dolly P. was visiting me on a weekly basis, out of guilt. One day I told her, That's all very nice, but I need to get out of here, and what can you really do for me? She said, There's talk of a time-stop, you know, like in the Middle Ages—why don't we wait a few days, see what's what. I said, Dolly, what the hell are you talking about? If you don't want to help me out, just say so. I knew how to work her. She said, What do you need? I said, A rope, a knife, a pickup truck. She said, I do this for you and we're even, that's it. I said, I get out, we'll talk.

1991, Part 2: The First Time-Stop in More Than a Thousand Years

The first thing people noticed when time stopped: clocks and watches. Nobody could bring back the ticking. Expert horologists from around the world were working the case day and night, except there was no day and no night, only a dim gray. With time went the date: calendars disappeared, the top right corners of newspapers were naked, and the postmarks on letters just said *Sent.*

Time Counters started emerging everywhere. They would stand in public places and count out loud: seconds, minutes, hours. They were determined to prove that time hadn't really stopped, that this was only a problem of counting mechanisms, and that humans had to step in and do the work until things got better. It soon became apparent that no one could reliably count time for longer than ten hours, so Time Counters formed teams and used special signals to let each other know when one Counter wanted the next to get ready. They were extremely meticulous, but really they were nothing more than singers of repetitive numbers. After a while, they began to fade away.

Dolly P.'s newspaper ran the story of my escape twice in a row, in successive dateless editions, then had me on the front page a third time. I understood, Dolly P. needed to cover her tracks, be the good reporter no one would suspect of any wrongdoing. But for a while every time a stranger looked at me I felt my muscles flex, getting ready to run. At some point it became clear that no one was reading the paper anymore; when people don't believe there's a future, they don't bother staying current. For the first time in a long time I thought, Maybe I can feel safe.

An Interval: The Time-Stop Stops

Eventually, it happens. A child sees a flower—maybe a lilac, or a rose—and insists that it has grown since he saw it last. He is young enough to notice.

The following day, a dog gives birth in some bathtub, to the amazement of her owners, who didn't realize she was pregnant. In a different place altogether, numbers appear on someone's pay stub: the date. Rumors start, and people grow optimistic, and with their optimism comes sundown, followed by sunrise the next morning. The last stubborn Time Counters faint on side roads, relieved of their duty, useless. For long days, beds are squeaking with hope, and a new generation is conceived.

As can be expected, regaining a state of normalcy is not a thing that happens overnight. A good example: when time resumes, women who've been trapped in inactive pregnancies give birth within forty-eight hours, regardless of how far along they were when time stopped. The babies almost always survive, but life is never easy for them, with their transparent skin and unfinished features; people call them the half-baked, and generally consider them to be not completely human.

And yet somehow, in spite of the half-baked walking among us, in spite of mad, ersatz Time Counters who walk the streets of our cities mumbling numbers, convinced that time has not resumed, in spite of the various inedible, temporally corrupted fruits and vegetables that the earth, after its long stagnation, produces for at least a year—people forget. People forget because they choose to do so, because remembering allows for the possibility of recurrence. People forget, and make cardamom tea, and fall in love, and buy ties. On Valentine's Day, they pay for overpriced dinners. Salmon in their mouth, they talk about their planned vacation for the summer. At weddings, they try to guess who the next person to get married will be, and they smile at the thought of the entire family together in one place *again*, the joy it will bring. Every moment, they wait for the next. Every day, they think about the future. They forget.

I can say this: I never forgot. I found it curious that people around me did. I remembered, and I knew that time would stop again, only to resume again, only to stop again. It seemed obvious, like gravity, or death.

2001: Phil

We met during the next time-stop, in 2001. By then I was a soaper; Phil came to see me in the Public Cafeteria, where I always held preliminary sessions with potential clients. These sessions were necessary because often people had different ideas about the kind of service I was providing. After the first misunderstanding, I realized I needed to take the time to go over the basics in advance: you will be cleaner than you've ever been, but there will be no sexual activity of any kind, that sort of thing. Given my past, I couldn't risk any confusions about illegal matters. Nowadays I charge for preliminary sessions, too, even though there's no actual soaping involved, but back then I had about ten regular clients and maybe six or seven here-and-theres, and I thought if I played too strict I wouldn't get new business. I was young. I didn't know yet that life usually worked the other way around.

At the Cafeteria, Phil looked at me, and right away I knew where things were going. It seemed pointless to waste time, so I said, You remind me of someone: a man I had an affair with. I do? he asked. Yeah, I said, only his eyes were different and he was Israeli and my officer in the army. He smiled. Was the sex good? he asked. Phenomenal, I said. He liked this answer, which was a lie: the officer's philosophy was, anything over four minutes is a waste of time. But men want to hear that sex can be phenomenal; it opens possibilities.

I figured, it's a time-stop; people do all kinds of crazy things. Once the clocks start ticking again, he'll remember that forbidden fruits aren't often worth eating and go back to his wife.

But it was my profession, not his wife, that brought up problems between us. Phil thought I shouldn't charge him anymore. I said, Then I can't soap you; it's against union rules. He said, That's just an excuse, you're not someone who'd let unions control her. Eventually, I agreed—though I really needed the money—but our problems didn't stop. Clients were just showing up at my door whenever they needed a soaping, since setting up appointments during a time-stop is practically impossible. Phil would get incredibly jealous every time I left him to tend to someone else. "Your hands all over his body" and all that bullshit. I said, If you want to be jealous, at least be original about it. He said, Bambi, believe me, I'm as original as it gets.

And he was. He was a strong man with a child's heart. Sometimes he would try to look tough, or even say something mean, but I would look at him and see he was only asking for love.

Clocks were still at a halt when I came home one day to find him collecting his things, stuffing socks and shirts into brown paper bags. I felt every muscle in my body stiffen, and not only because I didn't want him to leave; I'd told him my real name, which was something I very rarely did in those days—the law people weren't after me anymore, but you can never be too careful. I stood there and looked at him. Finally, I said, Look, I'm a professional soaper. That's what I do. What did you expect? This isn't about that, he said. You miss your wife? I asked. I'm not going back to my wife, he said. I don't understand, I said. I thought you were the one, you know that? he said; but lately I'm not sure. I have to be sure, Bambi. You have to be sure? I asked; I hoped that if I repeated it he'd realize how ridiculous he sounded. He looked right at me. This isn't working, he said.

For a while, I stayed in bed, ignored the bell when clients rang it. Soon after, time resumed.

2011, Part I: Phil's Return

All of a sudden, he came back.

Dolly P. offered to have a colleague run a soaping piece centered on me. We'll use stock pictures, she said, to be safe. You won't use my real name, I said, but I think real pictures are fine. After so many years with no one after me, I felt it was a small risk. And perhaps the truth is, we all forget the things we most need to forget; after living a careful life for so long, I was ready to believe I could be free. And I wasn't wrong—no law people showed up. The photo featured me with gloves on, scrubbing a woman's arm with a toothbrush. I enjoyed looking at it. And, apparently, so did Phil.

At the door he said, You haven't changed a bit. Time-stops will do that to you, I told him; I'm younger than I am. Actually, that's not accurate, Phil said; studies show that after time-stops, cells grow quickly, and the body makes up for lost time. Already we were arguing. And yet all I wanted to do was hug him; he was new and familiar and I realized how much I'd missed him.

I wanted to ask where he'd gone when he'd left ten years ago, where he'd been since, but predictable questions only lead to predictable answers. Instead, I offered watermelon. We could never share one when we were together, since fruits don't grow during time-stops; it was one of the few things I'd missed, in those days. It's my favorite fruit.

Phil and I sat on the floor and he popped the melon open. Red oozed all over the rug, and for a second I wanted to suck it all in, like a vacuum cleaner, like a madwoman. But I didn't, because by then I was old enough to know that most people can't tell passion from weakness.

The next thing that happened was happiness. It crept up on me then, for a short while. Mornings he cooked eggs, and I didn't have to remind him how I liked them. Evenings we talked and talked, letting words linger and thoughts carry their weight. Maybe this is love, I thought: losing the need to escape.

Then, two weeks in, I woke up one morning and my heart was beating hard. Phil was snoring peacefully in my bed. I shook him and said How did you find me. He said he called the paper, got hold of Dolly P., paid her to give him my address.

I said, Dolly P. doesn't need money.

He said, I never said *how* I paid her.

I said, There's an agenda, then, Phil. What's the agenda?

Sure took you long, darling, he said. I was waiting for you to ask.

This was Phil's idea: we create another time-stop. I thought he was being ridiculous, and that's what I said. He said, Bambi, don't play with me. I said, Don't call me that if we're not really a couple, if you're only here to get results. I was getting dressed now. He was watching me with sex in his eyes, saying nice things about my body, but it takes more than that with me. I said, Phil, you stop this and you stop this right now. I'm leaving—four hours is what you've got. The apartment is yours, use anything, call anyone. Make a proposal, a presentation, a pitch. It's business now is what it is, I said; you and I are done. When I'm back, you get one shot. You talk, I listen, I make up my mind and that's it.

I hoped he would say Bambi, what do you mean we're

done, forget this nonsense and come over here. What he said instead was Okay. He seemed ready, up for the task. I went to the park and sat on a bench. I tried to figure out how much he knew. Four hours is a very long time when you feel cheated.

What this man put together was remarkable. The photographs were what really got me: me, all over my apartment, blown up to a size a woman should never see herself in. Me, huge, in prison; me, huge, in Ashdod, the Israeli town linked to the whole bruchtussis fiasco; and the one that made me nauseated, me, even bigger, escaping. I said, How. That's all I could say, and I said it a few times. Phil was waiting, letting me take it all in.

Eventually he said, To save time, let's skip the bullshit. I know how you escaped from jail. I know everything, so let's not play here.

I hoped he was talking about Dolly P., about the pickup she got for me, the guard she bribed. But Phil's voice was telling a different story.

He said, It's maximum-security, Bamb, the best in the country. You really think I'd buy the bribe story and stop looking? Then he said, The bribe was only a decoy, right? I bet you didn't even need it. You just wanted the cops to find something when they came looking, so no one would find out you stopped time to get out. Right?

It was exactly right.

Did my feelings cloud my judgment? Sure. When you

love a man, it isn't some fanatical presentation that sways you; I was still hoping there was feeling at the bottom of things. But all in all I believe I had very little choice. This man had a map of my world.

Bambi, he said, I want you to do what you did in '91. I said, I can't, it's not something I control. He said Bullshit. I said Phil, it really isn't. It's a power that comes over me, that came over me then, not something I can summon. He said, You sure "summoned" it when you wanted your freedom back. The word *summoned* came out sarcastic and mean—meaner, I thought, than he'd intended.

I wanted him to understand. I said Phil, please listen now. One day in jail, I got this sensation. It wasn't the first time, it's been coming and going since I was very young, but I never knew what to do with it. It always starts with this slow internal tremble, and then my brain begins to feel like copper, and I know that if I tilt it to one side and concentrate it can float, it can do things. In prison, I couldn't stop thinking about my cat. I had a cat then, Keyvan, and every time I closed my eyes I would see Keyvan passed out, or trying to drink water from the toilet to stay alive. I needed to get to him. Then I talked to Dolly P. The bribe was like you said, but the rest was backup—I didn't know what would actually happen. And then when it did happen, it was as mundane as buying tomatoes. I tilted my head, and everything froze—the world froze. It was almost disappointing, how easy it was, the opposite of magic. But Phil—once I was out, people were moving again, and my brain just felt like a normal brain. And I've never had that sensation since. All right? Do you understand?

He was quiet the whole time I talked, listening intently. Then he said, You simply let it go once you were out. It was a choice. I said, Maybe, but it didn't feel that way. He said, For our purposes, it doesn't even matter; you let it go, it let go of you, whatever. Time had already stopped. You started something, but the world had the last say.

Phil's features softened suddenly. He took my hand, and I let him. Bambi, he said, you're so naïve. What about 2001? I asked. Did I do that, too? It was one of those things I'd always suspected but never let myself know. Phil smiled. It took me quite a while to figure that out, he said, but it doesn't matter now. You can stop time, Bambi, that's the important thing. And you're going to do it again, for me.

We spent the next few days discussing the plan. The first thing I wanted to know was why, why he wanted this, and Phil talked about "doing it right this time." There are opportunities, great fiscal opportunities in a time-stop, he said, and we were stupid then, in 2001, just staying in bed and having sex. He said "having sex" like it was the worst thing you could do with your time.

Once time stops, Phil said, waiting as much as possible is key. People grow so desperate that they forget how to hope, he said. They forget how passing time feels, and then there's so much more we can do for them. He talked about banking all the energy that the world saves, and the ways in which we could capitalize on that energy. Time capsules were one. Selling dreams was another. He was excited. It seemed like I wasn't getting the whole story, but I didn't know what part was missing.

An Interval: 1982, a Memory

There is a moment I remember well. I was twelve years old, discovering for the first time that desire made the air thinner. I was running in a field. This was in Israel, a field on the outskirts of the town where I grew up. It was wartime, but the kind of war not too many people cared about. Also in the field: boys and girls I went to school with, a bonfire. My clothes were all stripes: gray and black, a matching skirt and top I had gotten the day before. This is what I heard: a boy I loved, who had broken my heart a few weeks earlier, was now jealous because I had a new boyfriend, a decoy boyfriend, a boy I never wanted. The two of them were trying to figure out who had the moral obligation to step back. Other boys were there to supervise, make sure things didn't escalate to a fight. This is what I learned: boys think that life is a call they get to make. This is why I started running: overturning this boy's rejection made me feel too powerful, like life was a call I got to make. The smoke in the air from the bonfire got in my lungs, and I thought I would run forever.

2011, Part 2: Hope

I tried many times and nothing happened, but Phil never worried. He believed that it was only a question of time, that I'd get it eventually. He said rumors in the street had already started, which showed that my brain was releasing some kind of substance, just like in '91. More than anything, he wanted me to believe in my power.

Every few days I'd try again, and fail again. It was clear what the problem was—there was nothing at stake. I knew that hurt Phil's feelings, because it showed him his goals were not my goals. But he never complained. He had enough patience and confidence for both of us.

What happens when you don't complain is that solutions find you. On a Tuesday morning, after we'd made love, Phil lay next to me and said, Bambi, just relax now, can you do that for me? I said nothing, but he knew I meant yes. He did all kinds of things with his fingers then: nothing too sexual, just tapping, touching without touching. He said, Close your eyes, and when I did, it felt like I had a blanket. This went on for a while. Then he said, How about we do this, and when the time-stop is over we make a baby.

I never knew that this was what I wanted. But now I knew, and all of a sudden it was the only thing. My breathing hastened. That's right, he said. What do you say?

I had to ask now. What about your wife, I said. Long gone, he said, and then again, long gone, and the way he said it answered the question I hadn't asked. I knew at that moment that our first encounter had not been random; knew that he'd already had intentions back then, the beginning of a plan. Whoever he'd been with before me had probably become unnecessary to his plan, the way I almost had. I knew all that, but I didn't care. There was no effort left in me, except the kind that makes you get up in the morning to braid a child's hair, write a note for school.

The next day, time stopped again. I still experienced it as two entirely disparate events, in two different sites—my brain being one, the world another. But by now I knew better. Phil was the happiest I'd ever seen him. He couldn't stop talking. In our apartment, enthusiasm was everywhere, and in many ways we weren't part of the world anymore; outside, people were developing all the regular time-stop symptoms, reenacting patterns of behavior that were long ago declared detrimental, against studies and cold data, against the soft whisper of their own inner voice. At airports, riots were erupting. Airline company reps, and even the pilots themselves, would try to reason with the crowds; there was obviously no way to ensure safe travel, no way to synchronize sky traffic, and you'd think that people would understand that. Instead, they threw stones, broke glass, shouted things like "But I need to get to my convention, asshole."

On street corners, huge piles of microwaves grew, their frustrated owners unwilling to remember that at some point time would resume, that when others stepped back into their own kitchens and turned on cooking timers—casually, as if they'd always been able to do so—they, the people who were quick to discard, quick to give up hope, would form the famous ten-mile lines outside the various Baking Solutions stores.

This is the truth: there is no objective reason for time-stops to be as devastating as they are. For example: food can be tricky, sure, but no more people die of starvation during time-stops than at any other time (supplies always last until the manufacturing of Synthetic Food is in full force, and generally speaking, people are a lot less hungry). And not being able to travel by plane is limiting, yes, but in fact the difficulty of going anywhere else allows you to more fully be where you are. Really, the worst thing about time-stops is that they make people believe that time is something like oxygen.

Phil and I were working around the clock, so to speak. I followed every instruction he gave me. Together, we built a big device that looked like a satellite dish, and another one that Phil called the Medusa—a big silver ring with eight arms like hooks. Both fit in what used to be my study, after we took everything else out. The satellite dish, facing the window, was meant to receive much of the energy saved by the time-stop (up to 70 percent of it, Phil said proudly), and the Medusa was to store that energy and later convert it into a greasy blue liquid that Phil would use to make his products—mainly pills (those known today as T. pills) and these oddly shaped metal disks that allow some people to relive scenes from their old lives. (I personally see nothing but gray snow on my screen every time, which has been the subject of quite a few clashes between us—Phil believes that I'm blocking the feed on purpose somehow.)

We worked together, but it never felt that way; often I would shout out to Phil only to discover he was standing right next to me. I asked as little as possible about it all, afraid of the information as if it were another person lurking around the house. It was clear—this was Phil's main course, the one he'd been waiting for his entire life. I think he assumed I would come around eventually. I was waiting for him to be full, and trying not to resent him for his undying hunger. Waiting, when time is standing still, is not an experience I wish on anyone with a beating heart.

I used to be different; I used to find comfort in time-stops. I'd close my eyes and feel like I was in some underground maze; I couldn't get anywhere, but I wasn't supposed to. I try to remind myself of that every time I open my eyes to a new gray day. Still, I often forget.

This all happened a long time ago, though experts would argue that I can't technically say that. That's what it feels like, anyway, and I am now part of the Time Language Movement, so using these terms is a cause I spend my days fighting for. We believe in the power of language, and we believe that by using time expressions we can, at the very least, create an illusion of passing time so strong that it functions as the real thing in essentially every way.

Nobody in the movement knows about Phil, or about my involvement in what is now referred to as The Big One. I believe that, since we're all working for the same cause, none of that should matter. Phil, in turn, believes Language people are no different from Time Counters and other types of lunatics.

These days, he mainly operates from what he calls the Factory—a huge facility just outside of town, where they used to make cribs before everyone stopped needing to buy new ones. I know where it is, but I've never been there. If things between us were different, if I woke up one day and believed in his operation and wanted to do my part, I imagine he would take me over, give me the grand tour. I imagine he'd want me to fully understand the mechanics behind the dam that holds time back. I imagine he'd be happy. And some days I think Why not? Why not make him happy? But I know this: we are playing against each other in a staring match; if I look down, I have lost, and Phil will never change. And perhaps that's true anyway, perhaps I have already lost.

I still practice my profession. I rent a small bath at a Soaping Inc. downtown. They call me every time one of my clients shows up, and I usually drop everything and go. It's a good arrangement for me, given that I can't see clients at home anymore; letting strangers into the apartment is exactly the kind of mistake Phil would never make. If anyone ever knew enough to come looking, the files stacked in his study (once mine, then ours, now his) would expose everything. It sometimes seems that when I so much as look at them in passing, he can sense it.

There's no phone at the Factory, no way to reach Phil when he's there, and yet every morning before he leaves, he says, I'll be at the Factory, as if we're already a family, and maybe our daughter would have an earache and I would need him to come home.

Yesterday, we were sitting on the balcony, drinking champagne and eating crackers. The dim gray light outside was getting to me, the way it often does. I looked at the color of the champagne in my glass, then at the gray light, and again, and again. I was trying to concentrate so that one would somehow spark the other, but whatever gift I had, it's gone; I sold it for hope.

Phil said, Bambi, that's cute, what you're trying to do. He was mocking me, and it hurt, of course, but I've gotten used to this kind of pain. I looked at him. Sometimes he says unkind things but you can still see kindness underneath them. At the end of each evening, before we go to sleep, he goes to the kitchen and checks my vitamin jar, to make sure I've taken all my Nutrient Pills for the day. I said, What about what you promised me, Phil? What about the baby? I'd intended never to ask him that, but all of a sudden I forgot why.

He said, We'll get there, Bamb, we'll get there. When? I

asked. How about next year, he said, 2012? Pretending to set a date was his favorite joke these days.

I decided to try a different approach. Phil, I said, look at us. We have all the money in the world. Isn't that enough? It's enough, Phil, don't you see that?

I assumed that he'd feign agreement, let me relax; we both knew that he wasn't just making a profit, but also holding on as tight as he could, sitting on top of the whole still world without leaving our balcony. But he just sat there with a smile on his face that I'd never seen before, and seemed immersed in some conversation I couldn't hear. Finally, he got up, put the champagne glass down, helped a few crumbs slide down his pants. He looked down at me, and sternness took over the smile. I never understood women, he said, so smart and so stupid at the same time. I was waiting for him to explain, and then realized that he wouldn't, because he wasn't talking to me, not really. He was quiet for a few seconds, then said, Money? Money? For fuck's sake, Bambi, we're living here in your crummy little apartment and you still think it's about the money?

He took a deep breath that said my stupidity caused him great pain. His disappointment hung heavy in the air, and I knew this was the moment when Phil had given up on me for good. I wanted to drink all the champagne until it made me throw up, then drink some more. Money, Bambi, he said like he was the president of a great nation and I was the ignorant masses he was preaching to, is always, always, a means to an end. Remember that if you remember nothing else.

And with that he turned his back to me and walked into the living room. I noticed there were crumbs on his ass that he must not have been aware of, remnants of the crackers we ate. This would have bothered him, I thought. Phil is a very tidy man.

MAYBE IN A DIFFERENT TIME

I'd gone thirty-six years without donating blood, had made a name for myself in my community for being the only man who refused to donate even on leap years, when they pay more. Our town boasts the largest bloodbank in North America, and since the war, which started before anyone can remember, most folks around either work at the bank or donate for a living. My father took me to watch him donate when I was four. I didn't faint or cry like my friend Jordan F, like so many kids on their first viewings. I stood still and silent, narrowing my eyes at the nurse. When she was done, I asked for the tube. It's my dad's blood, I said, not yours. The nurse smiled, said, That's not how it works, honey pie. My father seemed frustrated; he'd explained the whole thing before we left the house. I squinted at them for a few more seconds, turned around and left the room.

In my twenties I had fire in my bones, something pushing me to teach this town some lessons. I can safely say the only people around who liked me were my sister and Jordan F. Everyone else thought I was a hippie or a bum, because why else would I not work in blood? But I never considered leaving. In my dreams, I was running for council and everyone was calling it a slam dunk.

Making a fortune seemed a good first step, so I tried my best. It's the money that wins the war at the end, not the blood, but no one around me seemed to know it. I made some good investments, learned to spot the investments that would later invest on their own. I can't say that I made a fortune, but for a while I was doing okay. Several times, I invited Jordan F to join in when I had a good lead, but he always coughed and said Thanks, I'm good. The truth was, my minor success made no difference; the town still looked down on me. Jordan F always stood by my side, but he managed to do that without risking his reputation. His job made it easy—people here respect the bloodtruck drivers, because at the end of the day everyone's hard work is in their hands, and because they are privy to more classified information than most. As Jordan F says, You can't drive with your eyes closed. But if Jordan F started investing with me, people's perception of him would change. And I guess I wasn't making enough money to make that worthwhile.

When times got rough, they got rough fast. I made some mistakes, then made things worse trying to correct them. It was a crisis of speed and faith, you could say—I was always a slow investor, always took hours staring at stats, and now that there was no time to do that, I found myself giving up and leaving, again and again, when all I had to do was believe that tomorrow's numbers would look better than today's. In short, I failed.

I needed cash, but for obvious reasons I tried to downplay my decision to donate. I didn't want everyone in town talking about it, speculating on the reasons. I went during the night shift, to one of the small stations on the outskirts of town, on a day when Jordan F was away delivering. I expected word would get out if I kept at it, of course; I just wanted to slow things down. What I didn't expect—couldn't have expected—was the rush that it gave me. No one had ever mentioned this lightness, all your worries losing their weight and the air getting thin like you're at the top of a mountain, close to the sky. Take more, take everything, I told the nurse, a woman whose braids I used to tug on years ago. Lie down, stop jumping, she kept saying, you've always been so restless.

I stayed up the whole night after that, awake with excitement. Suddenly I couldn't wait for Jordan F to come back, so I could share the news. The next day in the afternoon, I was walking down Benevolence Ave., which gets the worst of the town's traffic on weekdays. Through the sequence of moving-trucks and buses, a wounded man cried in an attempt to get my attention: Sir, sir, would you please lend me a hand? He was bleeding so bad it was hard to know which part of him was missing. The man was an out-of-towner, or at least I didn't know him. Our town always attracted that sort of thing—people assumed if we were donating blood, we'd be open to donating organs, too. Jordan F, anyone else in town, would have kept on walking. I crossed the street to get to him. He was begging—Please, man, please, please. His body contorted as if he were trying to draw something in the air with his knees. I looked at him and felt a tickle of the lightness from the previous night. I thought, He did say *lend.* And if he doesn't actually give it back, well, I'll still have the other one.

A few hours later I walked over to Boon's Bar a one-armed man, to meet Jordan F. My left pocket felt empty—I had the habit of twirling my fingers in there—but it was the kind of emptiness that didn't seek to be filled. When I stepped in, Jordan F noticed the change right away. And right away he was being judgmental. I said, Let me point out that I'm perfectly functional with one arm; most days I forget I used to have two. Jordan F snorted. Most days? he said; it's only been a few hours. It was one of those truths whose falseness you couldn't prove. I don't care to discuss this further, I said. The conversation I wanted to have felt out of reach.

All right, Jordan F said, but what's going on with you?

There's a rumor going around that you started donating. He said this with half a chuckle and all of a sudden I wished he'd go on a very long delivery. I did, I said and flipped him my donor stamp. Jordan F's eyes opened wide, and his mouth angled toward his chin. Why? he said, stunned. I needed the money, I said, my words quiet. I knew I'd been happy a couple minutes ago, but couldn't remember why. I thought that's what you always wanted, I said. Yeah, no, Jordan F said, I don't know. We sat there like that for some time, ignoring our beers. When we were younger, before Jordan F started driving blood, people used to tease us, call us faggots. Real friendship between two men is not something you see in this town. I never minded it much, but it used to bug the hell out of Jordan F. It's been so many years, but I found myself thinking about it now, sitting at Boon's with him.

I thought for a while that he would never speak again, or at least not to me. And even though I walked in thinking we would toast and laugh, a part of me knew it would go exactly as it did. Jordan F was always giving me grief for not donating, separating myself from the town, but he didn't really want anything to change. He liked that I knew nothing about bloodwork. When you've known someone your whole life, all it means when you feel surprised is that you're fooling yourself.

Shortly after, my sister, Lulu, needed a kidney. It got worse was all she said on the phone, but I knew what she meant—she'd been sick since we were small.

Jordan F and I had been distant since that night at Boon's, so I asked Lulu not to mention anything. Sure thing, Lulu said, which usually meant she wasn't listening. The next day, Jordan F was at my doorstep. You're saving the life of our little sister, he said, and you thought I would give you a hard time? She's not your sister, I said. Jordan F always loved Lulu, used to say when she smiles, armies around the world stop fighting. (Jordan F, due to his line of work I suppose, always talked about the war as if any pause in the fighting was a precious gift, more than we should expect.)

Look, I'm sorry I was an asshole, Jordan F said. If you want to start donating, you should start donating. Who am I to say? I was only surprised, he added, because I thought you'd ask me for money if you were short, that's all. His voice squeaked as it does when he lies, but I smiled. He was trying his best.

To donate a kidney, you had to belong to an organization; the organization issued a card, and I was put on a database. People from around the world started writing to me, sharing awful stories. I read and kept every letter, mainly out of superstition—I had a feeling that, the day I got rid of one, Lulu's body would start rejecting my kidney. But I only filed the letters and ignored them; I saw no point in writing back to disappoint. And I wasn't about to give away any more of my organs. Life had calmed down: Lulu was getting better, Jordan F wasn't mad at me—which mattered more than I cared to admit, more than it should have—and once a week I would go late at night to donate some blood and feel high. It was enough money to keep me going, and no one in town seemed to talk about it much. On the nights when Jordan F was home between deliveries, we would be at Boon's until the dark started to fade, and whenever Lulu was feeling up to it she would drive over and join us. We avoided any talk of blood or the war or donations, and for a while all of that was just fine.

When I got the letter from the woman in Uzbekistan, I filed it away with the rest, but it stayed with me. In my dream that night, she and I were sitting at the top of a mountain, playing card games. The game seemed to be whoever gets the king wins. I'll tell you what, the woman said in a British accent, if I get the king three times, you have to give me what I want. And if I get the king three times? I asked. No one will bother you again, she said.

I woke up and thought about it rationally. I'd never been a smoker. I was pretty certain I could do with one lung.

A reporter from a local paper a few towns over contacted me after that, wanted to run a story. You are an altruistic man, he said, and for a moment I let myself think perhaps I was, so I said Thank you. When he asked why I did it, I said this kind of giving made me happy. I said "It's a special feeling." I didn't describe the feeling. I avoided the word *high.*

The reporter used some Russian woman to pose as the Uzbekistani patient in the photographs, but all in all he did a decent job. And it was strange—reading it, I felt I was looking at a self of mine I hadn't known.

I expected an angry call from Jordan F. The story revealed I'd been a single-lung man for weeks, and I figured at the very least he'd be hurt I never told him. I also figured he'd have some things to say. He wouldn't be able to dismiss it as silly provocation this time, nor would he consider it justified as he did with Lulu. He might be outraged. He might tell me that he didn't know who I was anymore. He might say something worse.

When he called I took a deep breath and held the air at the top of my lung for as long as I could. Then I exhaled and answered the phone. I want Lulu to start going on deliveries with me, Jordan F said. Okay, I said, confused. Maybe he hadn't seen the article after all. You are her real brother, so I wanted to run it by you, he said. Okay, I said. It would still be a while before she'd go back to work, he said, and in the meantime the fresh air would do her a world of good. Okay, I said. I sat there for a long time after we hung up, feeling the weight of my body, the weight of all my organs, pulling me toward the ground.

A week later, my ex called—a woman I thought I loved once because her muscles were strong and her smile soft. I hadn't heard from Katrina since I broke up with her three years before, but Lulu claimed to have seen her once on a street corner, begging for money. She was a carpenter when we were together, but I guess when times got rough few people were spared.

On the phone, Katrina said I'd broken her heart. She needed a new one. She'd read the story about me and surely if I was helping perfect strangers whose wounds I hadn't caused, I would help her. I could tell she was reading from a note. Due to my broken heart, she was saying, I have been rendered unable to work, degraded to panhandling. Kati, I said, a heart's no small thing. You're not using yours anyway, Katrina said—her first spontaneous words in the conversation. She was clearly being sarcastic, but she made a valid point.

I knew it was a big decision, of course, but it felt small to me. Jordan F and Lulu were on the road, so I saw no need to share the news.

What I learned about charity was, word always gets around. People kept finding me. The woman with the facial reconstructive surgery gone bad was the next letter that got my attention. She used to be so beautiful restaurants paid her to patronize them. And perhaps, as Jordan F pointed out inside my head, beauty was not the thing to worry about in a time of war. I was often talking to Jordan F in my head. But,

I thought, that is what the woman is asking of me, that is what she needs.

Lulu called from the road that evening, said she couldn't tell me where they were but she was getting stronger with every passing day. It used to be that Jordan F went on long deliveries only when the fighting got worse somewhere and the demand for blood was especially high. How come you're away so long? I asked Lulu. You know I can't answer that, she said, but you can figure it out. Nothing's been reported, I said. That's not how it works anymore, she said; reporting risks lives. I held the phone for a bit, not knowing what to say. Then Lulu said, From what I understand, you work in blood now yourself, so what's with the war judgment? Let's talk about something else, I told her, and besides I only donate blood once a week, to get by. You know, she said, I keep telling J. that you know what you're doing; if you're donating organs, you're donating organs, we should still support you. But I see now what he means when he says you've changed. Please stop, I told her. I was starting to shake. If Jordan F has something to say, he should call me himself, I said, and hung up.

I wished our conversation had gone differently—I wanted to ask Lulu for her advice on the face-surgery woman. But it seemed there was no room for that kind of talk between us anymore. When I stopped shaking, I tried to think about things rationally. It is no secret that in our world a faceless woman is as good as dead, but a faceless man is still a man. Realizing this, I didn't see how I could say no. And looking back, I can say I wasn't wrong; my life didn't change much.

The only thing that did change was it seemed silly now to keep making a fuss. I knew if I was asked for something I still had, I would say yes. And I did—the alcoholic who needed a liver, the AIDS patient who needed my skin, the guy from Montreal who collected spleens for a living—I felt lighter with each part of myself I gifted. When a bomb fell in town—something that happened every few months, yet always got a good deal of attention—it seemed only natural not to wait till the requests came in. I walked over there to see what organs might be needed. It was warm out, and I was sweating by the time I got to the scene, so later, in the local paper, they said I ran over there as fast as I could and "gave everything I had to give." People appreciated it. Some called me the town hero. The difference between running and not running seemed immaterial, so I never mentioned it.

The highs were intense and usually lasted a couple of days, but I told myself that wasn't my reason for doing it. And as it turned out, I suppose I was right.

I got a letter from Jordan F at one point. I thought perhaps he'd heard I was helping people in our town and perhaps that changed his mind—Jordan F always valued loyalty.

I have one question for you, the letter said. Doesn't it feel like you're disappearing? I wrote back: No. It feels like I'm taking shape. I imagined Jordan F reading it, his face twitching.

It was only when that last request came in the mail, the one I had to refuse, that I was forced to look into myself. I was giving away my organs, but it wasn't out of charity, it didn't prove I was a good man. All it proved was I still had the one thing that mattered: my manhood. I felt ashamed realizing this, but I knew it was the truth.

The man's story was horrifying. He'd been away from home for nearly three years, fighting. On his first night back, his wife chopped his penis off in his sleep because she believed he'd cheated on her while away. I wanted to help this man so badly my balls hurt. It was as if they were already getting ready to relocate, stretching out toward a new body. I cried, coughed, couldn't stop saying no, no, no for hours. I sounded something like a miserable rooster. I couldn't breathe. It was clear: I couldn't do it.

For the first time in a long time, I debated contacting Jordan F and Lulu, who I could only assume by this point were more than just traveling together. I knew they would likely be supportive, say I was allowed to draw a line somewhere, I was entitled to my feelings. I didn't call. I tried saying these same things myself, but all I felt was sadness. I wanted to be a better man—the kind of man who's not a prisoner of his own anatomy, the kind of man who saves a life if he can, expecting nothing in return. A true hero. But ultimately, I failed.

Dear Sir, I wrote. Everything you've heard about me is true, but unfortunately I cannot help you, for if I help you it will be the end of me. I would never again be able to love another body, never be able to conceive a son, and if ever I wanted to fight for something I believed in, no war—neither the one we're in, nor any future one—would take me. I would be considered a man no more (no offense). Maybe in a different time, in a different world, I wrote. I could only hope that he was smart enough to know what I meant, and kind enough to forgive.

TZFIRAH

When the sun comes down on Tel Aviv, it comes down hard. You open a window and darkness is everywhere. You think, Wasn't this land lit up just now? Wasn't the air yellow only moments ago? But you can never be sure.

You flew in from New York when your sister was enlisted—of course you did—and her new olive uniform could have fit two of her. The induction center you were all escorting her to was attached to your old base, and in the car on the way over you waited for that familiar right turn onto a winding road. It's all straight after that, you remembered—straight through treeless, browngray streets with no U-turn. Your dad joked about how excited you must be. You put your hand on your sister's knee and pretended not to notice the shaking. Then: the waiting area that looked like a parking lot, your sister small like the drive had shrunk her, and a giant billboard of names blinking red. Your father was the first to notice when her name came up, and you felt angry at him for seeing.

When the sun comes down on Tel Aviv, it comes down hard, and on the days when people try to remember, it comes down even harder. In Israel, there are days devoted to the task of remembering. Once a year: remembering the Holocaust. Once a year: remembering fallen soldiers. This is how a nation achieves collective remembrance: it freezes to the sound of a wailing siren for the duration of one minute, or two. Cars stop mid-road, screaming babies go unattended, and if you turn on the television or radio you hear nothing but the soundtrack of grief.

Now here's the confusing thing: remembrance sirens sound exactly like wartime sirens. In Tel Aviv, this can get especially confusing if you are someone who currently lives abroad. If Tel Aviv is your hometown but on this Day of Remembrance you are merely visiting, this is what will happen to you: You'll be brushing your teeth, when suddenly you'll hear a gentle cry growing into something violent, the roar of a man-made wailing machine. You will think that maybe a new war is starting, or an old one returning, because the Gulf War is something that *your body* remembers, and sirens are part of that memory.

You were twelve, and for a while your family moved from city to city in an attempt to avoid danger, but the Scud missiles seemed to follow you. Finally you settled in a town called Raanana that seemed far enough from peril and close enough to routine: school for you, day care for your sister, work for your parents, every morning all of you clutching your boxed gas masks like purses. You got your first period in that temporary home, and in the bathroom which was not your bathroom you stared at the blood for a long time. Then: the siren; another missile was on its way.

Brushing your teeth, you will think about that war and say to yourself, *This is probably nothing.* A few seconds later you will open the bathroom door and shout to your sister, *What's going on?* But she will not hear you over the piercing sound of her music; on this Day of Remembrance, she is a soldier on her day off, trying hard to *forget.* You'll spit, and with toothpaste on your lips like foam you'll shout again, you'll shout loud. Your sister will hear you. She will step out of her room and gasp. This is what she will scream: *Tzfirah!* In Hebrew, the siren that reminds people to remember has a special name—Tzfirah.

You will want to laugh at the absurdity of the moment, but you will not. You will want to hug your sister with too much force and whisper, *Don't go back to your base*, but you will not. *Let's pretend we can't hear it*, you will want to say; *let's walk over to the kitchen, toast some bread, fry some eggs.* But you will not. For the remaining twenty seconds, this is what you will do: stand still alongside your sister, listen to the siren, and think about death, about darkness that takes over a city in a flash when the sun comes down hard.

BEEP

Everyone knows Thursdays are wacky. It was a Thursday when the new shopping center opened, when, thrilled by its proximity to my apartment, I spent some money on ceramic pots I didn't need. Also, a few books I already had but couldn't resist rebuying. I came home carrying bags of purchased happiness, but no one was there to share my excitement. And then I heard the beep.

I looked for the source of the beep everywhere: nothing. Under the blankets, behind the TV, inside the refrigerator: nothing. Every time I thought it was gone, it would beep again. I counted the seconds. My discovery: inconsistency. Five seconds, eight, two, twelve. Beep, beep, beep, beep. I stopped counting. I tried to convince myself it was one of those things that happen on Thursdays, no big deal. I wasn't buying it.

Jojo got home around seven. Hi, honey, I said, how

was your day? I was waiting for the first beep we could share. I was waiting for him to go crazy trying to figure out where it came from. Jojo was the kind of guy who would. I waited: no beep. More than eleven minutes: no beep.

Hungry, babe? Jojo asked, and went in the kitchen to fix dinner. No thanks, I said. And it beeped. Hear that, Jojo? Hear that? I shouted. I was excited. Hear what, babe? he shouted back. The beep, the beep, there was a beep, didn't you hear? I was mad at him for missing it.

Then I thought: Maybe it's my own private beep. Maybe it won't beep when Jojo's around. Weird, I thought—everybody usually liked Jojo. Then dinnertime came and refuted my theory. My beep was beeping all through dinner. Jojo was right there. He couldn't hear it. I asked, almost every time: he couldn't hear it.

Then: the particles. They were small at first, so I didn't mind them. Small particles flying through the air can be distracting, yes, but I've seen worse.

We were at a restaurant. Jojo, I said, did you see that? Then I asked the waiter, and a woman sitting at the next table. I was thinking there might be something wrong with Jojo. There wasn't. They couldn't see the particles either.

Then the particles got bigger, and then even bigger. Soon there were things flying in the air that could potentially be hazardous. For example: the stop sign that got knocked down by the storm the other day; an equestrian. Despite the danger, I felt relieved; my particles were part of something larger. I kept dodging: I had to. Jojo thought it was a twitch. He made an appointment for me to see a neurologist. Jojo, I said, there are fucking horses flying around in here. Babe, he said, you crack me up.

Then the strangest thing happened. Jojo came home from work one day, and he wasn't Jojo. He was Dora. He had breasts and everything. He didn't even look like Jojo, or sound like him. For three days, he denied it. Denied the breasts, denied the voice, denied the blond hair. Finally, she cracked. You're right, she said, I'm not even sure who Jojo is. That's it, I said to myself. Jojo's gone. I'd always known that one day he would leave me.

Dora couldn't see or hear any of it either.

One day Dora came home from work and said, We gotta talk. Babe, she said, you're seeing things, you're hearing things, I'm worried. Aren't you, I said, hearing things, seeing things? I gave examples. Babe, she said, it's not the same, it's stuff that's real. My stuff's real, too, I said. Who's to say what's real and what's not, I said. You're not being supportive, I said.

Dora said nothing.

Then I said: If that's really how you feel, I don't see this relationship going anywhere.

Dora said nothing once again.

We both said nothing for a very long time. Then the beep started beeping, Victorian chariots were flying in the air, and the ceiling was going up and down.

I forgot to say that sometimes the ceiling would go up and down.

Maybe you can try to see it, Dor, I said. My voice was very sweet. Loving.

Dora smiled.

I can try, she said, but I can't make promises.

That's fine, I said. That's all anyone ever does anyway. Try.

The first thing Dora saw was a dreidel. She said it was tiny, and purple. I couldn't see it. Then she said there were plenty of them, in all colors of the rainbow. It sounded beautiful. They were flying in all possible directions, she said, and they were too small to hurt anyone. Dora didn't have to dodge.

My mother was coming to visit. Dora and I were baking a cake. Dora said, Remember, babe, not a word. I used too much baking soda. I committed to memory: not a word, not a word. I knew I might still forget.

My mother's visit was the oddest thing. She kept calling Dora Jojo. Dora didn't seem to mind. That's fucked up, Dor, I said when we were in the kitchen and I thought my mother couldn't hear. I was wrong. What's fucked up, dear, my mother asked: standing in the doorway. I spilled the beans. All of it.

My mother said, Sweetheart, you are imagining these things, yes?

I said, No, Mom, *you* are imagining that you *can't* see them.

She said, Surely, sweetheart, you realize that you're bored. When you were young you used to try to fly. That was out of boredom too.

I don't remember that, I said; that's pretty stupid.

Actually, you pulled it off once, she said, but that's hardly the point.

My mother made hot chocolate, cut the cake. Then, on the sofa, she was stroking my hair: her attempt at making me hopeful. That's rather annoying, she said all of a sudden. What is, I said. Something is beeping, sweetheart, she said. Can't you hear it?

MY WIFE IN CONVERSE

I.

My wife and I took a cooking class recently. My wife and I take classes. It is a passion of my wife's, taking classes. My wife is good at most things one could take classes in, which, when you think about it—and I've thought about it—means my wife excels in all things. And I believe that is in fact true. I believe my wife excels in all things. I am not blinded by love when I say this—we have been together eight years. They say after seven, whatever blindness you had is gone.

While my wife was chopping things or perhaps sautéing them, the instructor came over. I stopped what I was doing, which wasn't much. He was a man in his sixties trying hard to look French. He smelled like years of garlic. We looked at each other until some time passed. You might want to take up poetry, he said finally.

2.

The poetry class conflicted with the cooking class—the one my wife was excited about, the one from which I was now banned. I make curtains for a living, and most of the work is done from a tiny shop I set up in the back of our house. In other words, my schedule is flexible; this sort of problem never happened before. What do you want to do? I asked my wife. In my chest I was hoping she'd say we both quit. I was imagining her saying, Intro to Tarot Card Reading. Or: I heard of a place, just a short drive north, where you can take horseback-riding classes. My wife loves intro classes, and loves anything that's a short drive north. But instead she said, We are not one person, you know. My wife had never pointed that out before.

3.

The poetry class was led by a young man with too much gel in his hair. His bio listed literary journals with exotic animals in their names, and words in Latin. I'm a poet before I'm a teacher, he told us the first day, a poet before anything. Everyone nodded.

4.

How was the cooking class? I asked my wife when we both got home. Dominique thinks I should open my own place, my wife said. After three classes? I asked. Eventually, she said, emphasizing each syllable. She looked at me like I had something on my face, but I knew that I didn't.

5.

Later that night, I went to my shop and cleared a small corner of my sewing table. In this corner, I thought, I can be a poet before I'm a curtain maker.

6.

Since then, every night I sit myself down, because that's the first step to anything worthwhile. I bark at myself from a dog place in my brain, a place only I can hear: Write! Then I get up and go to the kitchen to get some olives.

7.

The poem is about my wife, I think. The poem is about Sunday mornings, when the sun is too early. The poem is about being the last human being on earth, but responsible for someone else.

8.

Of course we still have sex, my wife says.

9.

The last time we had sex, it was cold out and they said a storm was coming. My wife was shivering in fear, making lists to steady herself. For a while I was trying to cross things off her list—candles, eight gallons of water, move things away from windows. Check, I would say cheerfully at her, check check check. But the more I crossed off, the longer the lists got, and the more anxious my wife seemed. She was sitting on our bed, her upper body low like it was trying to reach her knees. I stood close behind her, put my hands on her shoulders. Honey, I said, and she tilted her head back and looked up to meet my eyes. There was such fear in her face, and I hadn't thought this through; *Honey* was all I had. I said Honey again, to buy a few seconds, and then I just saw it, saw in her eyes the thing she needed to hear, saw it the way you see anything—a car in the driveway, a coat in your closet. I *promise you* it's going to be okay, I said; can you trust me? She let her head lean farther back until it touched my stomach, and I held her like that for a bit, then turned her around to face me, kissed her eyes. Her body softened, opened.

When the winds came later that night, they were far weaker than expected, and we were still inside each other. It had been a while since we made love like that—hearing our rhythms without effort, reaching toward each other without haste, again and again.

When we woke up the next day, the outside was yellow and brown, a strange mix of relief and disappointment. I tucked a curl behind my wife's ear. We didn't die, I said, and smiled. Don't be dramatic, she said, and got out of bed. God, I need to brush my teeth, she murmured with her back to me, heading to the bathroom; I woke up with an awful taste in my mouth.

10.

I like saying *my wife* to strangers, seeing their eyebrows twitch. The eyebrows always twitch. The only difference is whether they let them twitch or try to keep them from twitching because they're liberals. When they ask—smiling, to show they never twitched at all, why would they?—How long have you been married? I say, We were in the first weddings, Massachusetts. I nod a couple times and look away. If

I let myself see their eyes, I will see the next question. And I admit: I want to leave them to their twitching.

11.

Someone, perhaps my wife, used the expression *in conversation.* The street was being loud right as these words left her lips—loud on the end, loud on the *ation. In converse* was what I heard. I can use this for my poem, I thought. That is how I operate these days, like a thief.

12.

Whenever my wife wanted to read the poem, I'd say It's not ready it's not ready. Sometimes she'd say Read it anyway, read to me while I cook. Then I'd say I prefer to finish it first, and my wife would make a face. I didn't know why she felt this urgency with the poem. What I did know was: when it's ready, I want her to listen without cooking. I'd say nothing though, because what's the point?

13.

Last week in class we workshopped a poem written by an older woman with thick black hair. The teacher talked about mastering the quiet, which has something to do with space breaks. This woman is very good at space breaks, if I understand it correctly, and is quite close to mastering the quiet altogether.

After class, I collected my things slowly, waited for people to leave. The teacher was texting or perhaps checking his e-mail. I waited for him to make eye contact, and when he did, I asked How do I know when a poem is ready. The teacher sighed. A poem is ready when the poet stops writing it, he said. So I should just stop writing it? I asked, confused. The teacher put the phone in his back pocket. I said the *poet*, he said. He looked at me for a few seconds, then started moving toward the door. With his back half to me he said, Look, it's not personal, I just don't like it when students get ahead of themselves. Whatever poem you're talking about—let's workshop it first and take it from there.

I stood in the empty classroom for a long moment after he was gone.

14.

When I got home that night, I could hear laughter. I stood outside our door and listened. Why would Dominique be in our living room? But I was wrong—the laughter was coming from the kitchen. They were giggling at the salmon. My better half is home, my wife said when I opened the door, glancing in my direction. How am I better, I wanted to ask, in what way? I have an order to finish, I said and walked toward my shop. I'm sorry about the smell, my wife called after me; let me know if you need your pills. I'm allergic to fish, and sometimes the smell alone burns my lungs. It's a big order, I shouted back, I just have to finish it. I sat myself down and tried to find the quiet in my poem, but everything was loud. I tried to find the quiet in my poem until through the loudness I heard Dominique leave.

In bed, my wife mentioned a cooking seminar in the south of France. I can learn *so much* over there that I can't learn here, she said. I nodded in the dark. But there's more to learn here too though, I said. There was nothing before my wife said, Sure. When I heard my wife sleeping, I said, I'm quitting the poetry class. That's too bad, my wife said, already in a dream. It'll get too soggy if you soak it overnight.

15.

I didn't know the seminar was only a few days away, didn't know my wife and I had agreed she should go. I only understood the next day, when she brought the big suitcase up from the basement. She looked at my face and said, You didn't think I would take the small one, did you? It's a long time! I said No, of course, of course. I wanted to ask how long exactly, but got the feeling I was supposed to know. I didn't want to say anything that would make her think once again I wasn't listening. It was true—I was lately finding it hard to listen.

My wife cooked for me that night. Do you like it, she kept asking, even though I said a few times that I did. She was saying things about the texture of the food, and I nodded. I wanted to ask if she would still have vacation days when she returned. I'd been wanting us to go somewhere, but she could never take time off. Now, from what I understood, she was using those accumulated days for the seminar. But perhaps not all of them, I thought. Perhaps she would still have a few left? If she'd resist, I would say something like *If you can take time off for cooking, why not take time off for us?* I was thinking it through while chewing. I had good ideas, but the words stayed in my mouth.

Before my wife married me, she was married to a man. He liked his shirts ironed and his blankets tucked, which were two of the things they didn't see eye to eye on. On our first date, I took my wife on a boat—one of the ones that go around the city making everything look pretty. Even though she was still married, I already knew she would one day be my wife, so I planned well.

They say the past is the best predictor of the future, and what I say back is that it's actually the other way around:

the future, if you work hard enough at it, slowly changes your past. But there are times, and that night on the boat was the first, when I look at my wife and for a fast moment see that she belongs to no one, not even herself. She is always leaving someone.

16.

I'm sorry this is happening so fast, my wife said. She was all packed, and Dominique was picking her up in an hour. I wasn't sure what she meant; it didn't seem she was talking about the seminar. Well, you don't control the schedule, I said and tried to smile, and her chest dropped. I took a deep breath. Is he picking everyone up, I asked. No, my wife said. She was looking straight at me; that was the question she wanted. Are you meeting the others at the airport, I asked. No, my wife said. Everything was quiet then, very quiet and still, and it seemed the world would be that way for a while. We're hooking up with them at the resort, my wife said finally.

Even Dominique's car horn was quiet, a small bee in the distance. I do love you, my wife said with one hand on her suitcase. She kept her lips on my cheek for a bit.

17.

After my wife left, I slept for two days. My dreams were mostly about money: I was making a lot of it now. The curtain business took off, or I joined a start-up at just the right moment and made CEO, or, in one dream, I became a successful lawyer. And in all the dreams I was either showing off my new money to my wife, who was no longer my wife, or trying to win her back with it. In some dreams we were still together, and I was buying her diamonds and making her quit her job. I would wake up between dreams, sweaty and puzzled. My wife never complained that the curtain business wasn't making enough. My wife loved her job. My wife hated diamonds.

18.

When I got out of bed, I walked straight to my shop without brushing my teeth. I erased my poem, except the line I stole: my wife in converse. Then I took the pile of papers and marched over to the dining area by our kitchen. I stood there for a moment, holding my papers, and looked at the large mahogany table no one would be dining on for some time. The shop is for curtains, I thought, not for poems. Maybe that was the problem all along. Now, in this new space, I would start all over again. And this time I would get it right.

PHONETIC MASTERPIECES OF ABSURDITY

Sometimes after the men leave, Nadine's body tells her to wait awhile for the water. *Make that bath count more.* She lies still, and her skin feels too tight on her bones, like someone gave her the wrong size. With a finger that smells of them, she looks for sharpness where she knows she will find it: elbows, knees, shoulder blades.

The edges of her bones comfort her, but it's a feeling that passes quickly, and soon there is need for more, for *proof.* So Nadine gently touches her cheek with her knuckles; her knuckles are her secret weapon. She thinks: *These knuckles could make a peach bleed.*

She should probably charge more by now, but she can never figure out what to say, or how to say it.

The men smell of baby carrots, because their five-year-old son mistakes baby carrots for candy, and of sweat, because they are always nervous when they see her, even if they've been coming for years. Or they smell of ice cream, because last night their wife tried to revive the marriage with some innovative foreplay, and have Viagra breath, because they stopped trusting their body long before it failed them. It doesn't matter.

Thursdays are the busiest. She never understood why. On Wednesdays, her BlackBerry keeps buzzing with men's anticipation until she feels like there are bees inside her ears. So on Wednesdays, saying *no* is important. *I miss you, too, Baby; really wish I could.* Every man is Baby, no exception; that she learned early on. Even the sophisticated ones appreciate the gesture: the implicit warmth, the promise of anonymity. But she does know their names, of course, sometimes even their last name, and on a few occasions the name of a wife, a mother, a sister they haven't spoken to in six years. It pains them, that the sister won't return their calls. They ask, *Why won't she fucking let it go already?* Nadine doesn't want to look for answers. If they insist on talking, she touches their hair, lets her eyes scroll up and down their torso; she waits for their body to remember what it wants. Really, she waits for the chatter to stop, but the trick is still giving it the space it needs. Once, when it was absolutely necessary, she made tea.

Generally speaking, she remembers more than she should: the bump on the back of their neck, the sweat behind their ear right before they come, the scar on the toe of their left foot and the story behind it. There is always a story behind it. They tell the stories and then retell them. Because, well: if she doesn't truly exist, surely she doesn't remember; they desperately need to believe that she isn't real. But then there are times when she can see sadness in their eyebrows, in their lower back, and suddenly they want her to remember. Temporarily, they acknowledge her presence in the world. *It's funny, but you are the most stable thing in my life, you know?* In these moments, she has learned, a nod goes a long way.

The woman, the photographer, Mia, has been dominating her thoughts. Now Nadine even dreams of her. Last night, Mia was elected World President.

Nadine wants to know things like what's Mia's favorite fruit, what she looks like when she cries. *Mia.* She rolls Mia's name on her tongue until she sounds like a cat. Mia wants to know her, too: the first thing she said was *I'd like to get to know you, if you'd let me.* But Mia wants to know her the way a painter wants to know her canvas. Besides, there is always a lens between them.

Mia reached her through a friend of a friend of a friend, someone Nadine hadn't talked to in years. On the phone, Mia sounded aggressive, and Nadine wanted to say, Sorry, I don't think I'm interested. But for a few minutes she chewed the words like she chews her gum before falling asleep, unable to spit. Finally she said, *Okay.* She said it softly, and Mia didn't hear her, so she had to repeat. *Okay.* Nadine assumed they would meet at some bar or café. *I work on the Lower East Side*, she told Mia, *plenty of places to choose from.* But Mia said it would be helpful, for the *project*, if she could see Nadine's apartment. She may have used the words *natural environment.* As in: *seeing you in your natural environment.*

Nadine cleaned her natural environment even though it was already clean. She bought a new plant for the spot between the TV and the sofa that always looked naked. She made cupcakes, but also got cheese and wine, because she wasn't sure what the occasion called for. And all the while she was asking herself why she cared so much. People never want to come all the way up to Washington Heights, and there weren't many people in her life these days anyway, so maybe that's all it was, she wasn't used to hosting. But then, in the shower, where her thoughts are always honest, a different answer came: it was the word the photographer kept using. *Interview.* As in "Last week, Madonna sat down with us for an interview . . ." or "In a recent interview, the secretary of state expressed her concern . . ."

I'm conducting interviews with a few women—pretty long, thorough interviews, the photographer said in an accent Nadine couldn't quite place, the words going fast and their ends hard, *and then, you know, hopefully I'll find the best fit for the project, and hopefully she'll want to go ahead and work together . . .* She laughed what must have been a nervous laugh, but it didn't sound nervous, and Nadine would later learn that nothing Mia did appeared nervous. If the photographer chose her, Nadine would be photographed and then, *if all goes well* (Nadine wasn't quite sure what that meant), the photographs would be on display at some gallery for the world to see. In the shower, Nadine imagined an old Jewish couple, a young babysitter, a professor at Columbia; they were all at the gallery, looking at Nadine's body in the pictures, and even though Nadine had never met them, they now possessed an intimate knowledge of her, because that's what photographs do, isn't it? *Reveal.*

A photograph: Nadine is standing in her small kitchen, waiting for the water to boil. There's a yellow and tired quality to the room. Her back to the camera, Nadine is looking to the side, the left half of her face visible. She is about to make tea for herself and for Mia: green ceramic cups to Nadine's right, empty and waiting. There is nothing suggestive in the picture, nothing that tells the viewer how Nadine earns a living. What you can see is something like disappointment, and this you can see in Nadine's posture and, if you look closely, in her facial expression. Nadine is disappointed because Mia *already* has her camera out. All that clicking. How can you talk to someone who just click-clicks all the time? How can you get to know someone who reaches for the camera every time she feels something? You cannot. There is a brief moment in which this understanding sinks in, and the camera captures it.

Sometimes Mia forgets to ask permission. She moves things in Nadine's apartment to better situate herself—the couch, the seashell sculpture, even the TV. Nadine tenses when Mia touches the sculpture—it was made especially for her, years ago, by a man who could make anything with his hands, a man she hoped to marry—but when Mia lifts the TV with ease, Nadine feels light. She smiles, but another thing Mia sometimes forgets is to smile back. This happens when she is deep in thought. Then she catches herself. The knowledge that she was rude always passes through her like a wave, sudden and tall. By now, Nadine knows to wait for it: something like sadness in Mia's eyes, and then her spine curves, which looks a bit like she is shaking something off. Then the laughter, quick. Then, sometimes: *What can I say, I'm Israeli, aggressive by nature.* The only other Israeli Nadine knows is a client, a man who sells rugs on Long Island for a living. He is gentle and weak and likes to be pinched hard.

When Mia pushes the limits, *Would you be comfortable taking some of your clothes off,* she looks at Nadine with soft eyes that say *I will look at you all the way to yes.*

Maybe next time, Nadine says, because she doesn't want the eyes to stop.

One thing she wishes she could explain to Mia: she doesn't mind the moans. Or more honestly, though this embarrasses her: the moans are her favorite part. When seeing a client for the first time, that is what she's curious about, and she waits for that one moment, when the animal in him speaks to her. When the moment comes, she listens carefully—through the sound, through the exhale of it. There is information there, *knowledge*, for her to collect. She does. Later, when she uses this knowledge, the men moan more deeply, openly, air coming out through their throats, their teeth, their pores. This reveals more information, and so on, and so on.

She has something like a playlist in her brain; double-click on a man's photo and you can hear the sound he makes. How can she explain—to Mia, to anyone—that she understands these moans better than she understands words?

When people speak, they say things like: *It is what it is*, and *I believe her, but I also don't believe her.* Ridiculous, absurd things. But with sound you get something that language can't hide. With sound, you get the feeling underneath the words.

Feeling, for Nadine, is the place you go to when nothing makes sense. For example: a night spent on a beach, a man with salt in his hair and hands of magic, a man she loved. She said *This is the end, right?* And he said *Not even the beginning, Deenie.* As it turned out, they were both right.

All of Mia's questions are the same question. Something something sex worker something something choice something. Nadine always pauses before she answers. It appears as if she is thinking hard, she knows that. But the pause is the time when she says with no sound, *Ask me something real.* Every time, she waits for Mia to hear. When Mia doesn't, Nadine answers.

Would you mind repeating that, Mia asks sometimes; *I'd like to record you.*

A recording:

No, it's not that I don't *like* the question, it's just . . . easy to be seduced by the idea of "what if." You know? So I try not to do that.

Pause.

Sure I think about it, yes. I'd have made a good social worker if I stayed in school, I think. I'd have helped people. I mean, as I've said before, I think I am helping people. But maybe I'd have helped more that way, and maybe I'd have enjoyed that job more. And I wouldn't feel . . . I'd be more proud. Of what I do. And I'd have more friends, probably. I had some good friends in social-work school. But when I dropped out and started . . . working more, we just lost touch.

When Mia is recording, when the camera is away, she is listening. Nadine wants to talk minutes and hours, talk until there's no way for Mia to leave, talk until the buses have stopped running. One thing she hates about New York—the buses never stop running.

A moment: Mia and Nadine are eating, sitting on the floor. (*Can we take a break?* Nadine asked. *I'm hungry.*

Of course, of course, Mia said, but kept shooting.)

Nadine is thinking maybe she should leave the furniture in the other room like that for a while, maybe she should eat all her meals on the floor from now on. Something about it feels like a fresh start. She wants Mia to say nice things about the quiche she made, and when Mia doesn't, Nadine asks, and the sound of her own voice is soft, too soft. *How's the quiche? Good*, Mia says without looking up. Then she nods a few times. What did she expect Mia to say? This quiche has changed my life? And if she said that—if she looked right at Nadine for once and said, Is it possible for a quiche to change someone's life? Because I think this is the best thing I've ever put in my mouth and nothing will be the same after this moment—what would Nadine do?

How old were you when you moved here, Nadine asks, but she forgets the question mark. She sounds like she's demanding something of Mia, and, expectedly, Mia asks back, *Why? No reason*, Nadine says, *just curious*, and Mia says, *Let's talk later?*

Later, while Mia is going over her shots from the day, or that's what it looks like she's doing, she suddenly says, *I was nineteen*, and Nadine doesn't ask, because she knows what question Mia is answering, but still Mia says—somewhat impatiently, too—*When I moved here. You asked me earlier.* Nadine nods, tries to think quickly what to ask next. *You left school over there to come here?* she asks. If she allows even a moment of silence, Mia will announce Back to work, in that voice that's just an octave too low, the voice of relief.

No, Mia says, *I left the army to come here, or really came here because I left the army; I needed to get away.* Nadine doesn't understand, and she instinctively tries to hide it. She's a pro, there's a thing that she does with her eyebrows—it's not a nod, which would feel like a lie, and yet it's always enough, with the men, to make them believe that she got it, that no explanation is needed. Mia stares at Nadine's eyebrows.

That's what kids over there do after high school, she says, *become soldiers.* Nadine feels heat in her face, she knows she is blushing, although she never blushes, hasn't blushed probably since fourth grade, but she is blushing now because Mia knew that she didn't understand, knew that an explanation *was* needed. And inside her embarrassment she senses a kind of thrill, a thrill she never expected, the thrill of being caught in a lie. There's a brief pause; what words can follow the word "soldiers"?

So all the kids are recruited, Nadine says finally, *girls, too?* And Mia nods, says, *Yup*, keeps nodding. After a few seconds she adds, *Women do two years, men three. Oh*, Nadine says again. She wants to ask Mia what it means that she "left" the army—how can you leave if you're recruited, did she escape? But she knows she can't ask that, and yet she can't think of anything else to ask, although this silence has an edge to it, the recognition in both of them that this conversation is about to end before it really started.

I need to reload the film, Mia says. *Would you mind making some tea?*

Nadine wants to find the joke.

The first line is: A prostitute and a photographer walk into a bar. The punch line is: Tea. She doesn't have the rest yet, but still she laughs every time. For a few seconds she can think, What is this thing, it's absurd, it's *funny*. And it is, just then, for a short while. It is funny, and she feels relief in her muscles. She can move her neck without feeling the stiffness.

This happens only once and happens quickly: Nadine gives Mia a massage. Mia is stiff after a long day's work—Nadine recognizes the stretching of the neck sideways, a thumb searching for pressure points. What comes over Nadine? She doesn't ask anything. She crosses the room, stands over Mia, who's sitting on a chair, says *Let me help*. Does she wait a beat, give Mia a chance to object? Not really. There's something in Nadine's fingers that can heal, and when Mia realizes that, *feels* that, everything may change. So Nadine reaches for her. Mia's skin is soft, and she smells a bit like detergent, not what Nadine expected, but Nadine can't focus on that now, only on the knotted bones. She goes deep, could go deeper if Mia let her, but Mia doesn't relax into her touch, not completely. Mia is quiet. Nadine wants her to moan, is sure she would if she let herself, and she wants to say something, *Don't hold it all in.* But she doesn't. This is borrowed time, she knows, and anything could make it end faster; better not to take risks. Then, for a brief moment: Mia lets go. Her muscles soften in Nadine's hands, and this sensation makes it hard to remain steady, but she does. She uses her knuckles, rows into Mia, and Mia makes a small sound then, a sigh so low anyone else would have missed it, but Nadine doesn't, and into this sigh Mia says, *You're good.* Does Nadine imagine these words? No, Mia says them, and right after she says them she realizes what she said, her muscles realize what she said. How long does the whole thing last? No more than four or five minutes, probably. Mia gently moves forward, stretches, says *Thank you, that was so helpful.* Nadine stands there, her hands holding air, looking at Mia's back.

Everything/nothing happens once again, she is maybe losing her mind probably losing her mind has probably already lost her mind. Otherwise what is this. Maybe it's simple a feeling is all maybe just a bit different because it's a woman maybe a different part in her body flutters maybe the beat of the fluttering is different but is that all that is not all. Everything/nothing is how she thinks of it she has no words not even sound. Everything is right there in your hands but it's like water so nothing is there in your hands in moments it's gone and you say was it here? It was here it wasn't here it was here. One moment here it is I am not making it up not imagining and the next moment is upside down all upside down your hands are empty and you think stop stop stop. But the feelings are so strong so fast so quick they do what they want like: lightning thunder thunder lightning lightning lightning.

She practices, out loud, before Mia's next visit.

So—how did you get out of the army . . . ?

Do you ever think about living in Israel again?

You know, I've been thinking. Maybe if I could ask you some things, if we talked not just about me, this whole thing would feel less strange, more . . . balanced.

I think it might be good for the project.

So . . . have you ever been with a woman?

Or, um, even just attracted to a woman?

Do you think it's possible to be gay for just one person? Or for just a few?

Because, you know, usually I'm not attracted to women, but sometimes I am.

I'm just not attracted to that many people at all, I guess.

So when I am . . . it's kind of powerful sometimes.

I think I might be in love with you.

I'll be gone for a bit, Mia says. *I'm going to Israel to shoot.* Nadine doesn't say anything, doesn't move. *This trip was scheduled months ago*, Mia says, *it's for another show I'm working on.*

Something in Nadine's body is twitching—it is gentle like a heartbeat and she doesn't wish to make it stop, only to locate it, only to touch it. She touches the wrist of her right arm, then the left, then her neck in the place where you feel the swallow. She knows this must look strange to Mia, it is strange, but the thing keeps hopping around in her body, or else she has no idea what's happening. There is a clear sensation, everywhere and nowhere.

You feeling okay? Mia asks. Nadine nods, stops searching though the heartbeat doesn't stop. Mia is looking for her eyes but Nadine keeps looking away. *You know*, Mia says, *I wanted to thank you.* Nadine looks right at her now but keeps her face frozen. *This project, the other project, it's about soldiers in Israel, and I've been working on it a long time. It's been dragging.* She pauses now, smiles a smile Nadine has seen before but not often. She is so beautiful. Nadine feels the urge to look away but she knows she can't, not again, not right now. She doesn't smile back, and she can see Mia's confusion clearly, what to do with this new Nadine, where has the eager pleaser gone. But she goes on. *Our talk the other day helped me*, Mia says. *It reminded me why I started this project to begin with—the other project, I mean. You don't have to keep saying "the other project,"* Nadine says. Mia ignores her. *It's so normal in Israel*, Mia says, *the idea of the military, of everyone being part of that military, a country of soldiers. Eighteen-year-old kids getting M16s, being* trained, *and no one sees how fucked up it is. It's, like, "What choice do we have," "we're surrounded by enemies," all that stuff. And for years I've been wanting to shout: But can you still* see*? Necessary or not, can you* look at it*? Because, well, this is all very personal to me. I'm named after a war, did you know that? My name is the initials, in Hebrew, of the Yom Kippur War. My mother was pregnant with me when my father died, so she named me after the war that took him away.* Mia pauses now, looks down. *But then . . . I'm not even sure when, but at some point I stopped seeing it,* she says. *I mean, I grew up there. It's all so . . . familiar. The past few years I'd go and shoot and talk to these soldiers, these* kids, *and I'd leave every time thinking, What did I want to show again? It was like I forgot. But you—you reminded me. I think it was how shocked you seemed at the idea of mandatory service,* Mia says, *or maybe it was just talking about it; I don't often talk about it. So thank you,* Mia says, *for reminding me that when people hear about it for the first time, they're* disturbed. *It's like I have my eyes back on now.*

You're welcome, Nadine says.

How strange, to hear Mia speak so many words.

It takes some distance from Mia, hours and days spent without her, for Nadine to hear more fully what was said. She's on the A train home late at night, alone in a fast-moving car, when she understands. Mia was thanking her for her ignorance.

It's not easy, trying to get rid of a thought like that, and when Nadine tries, the opposite happens, a cramp in her stomach and a new thought, a worse thought, a word:

disturbed. That's what she is to Mia, isn't it? She's the soldiers, the thing you see every day but don't see, the thing you pretend is normal even though it's sick. The disturbance.

At the end of their last session, Nadine is sitting on her bed, knees to her chest, closing her eyes so as not to hear the clicking. She makes her fingertips remember touching Mia—the back of her neck, her shoulders—while she makes the rest of her imagine how tomorrow will feel.

Nadine's closed eyes accelerate the clicking; Mia is seeing, it seems, something she has never seen before. And she must be touched, because she is doing what she does when she's touched—she clicks.

Mia leaves that day like she's going out for milk. *See you later,* she says.

Mia's words on her voice mail months later are garbled. Nadine hears June 5th, hears 6 p.m., hears *really, really hope you can make it.* Listening to Mia's voice again, Nadine feels like she's looking at an old photograph of herself in which she's wearing clothes she never owned and someone else's face.

At the gallery, after hours on a Wednesday, Nadine is standing erect looking at herself, and herself is looking right back at her from the wall. *The opening was wonderful, I was sad you couldn't make it,* Mia says. And then: *Everyone wanted to meet you.*

She looks at Mia straight in the eyes then, and there is a feeling deep inside her, the pull of a magnet toward metal. It is hard—physically hard—but she resists the pull. She sees Mia's need to reach for the camera, to click the moment away.

So . . . on to the next project? Nadine asks. *Not really*, Mia says, shakes her head lightly. And then: *I'm kind of exhausted.* Mia seems to be saying something, and this is the kind of moment that used to get Nadine's heart beating faster with potential. If only she asked the right thing the right way, if only she managed to open the moment, reveal what's inside. *Well, you've been working hard*, Nadine says. Mia nods but looks down, says nothing at first, then: *I'm never exhausted from hard work.* She's definitely trying to say something. A small voice inside Nadine is whispering, *See? It's always been here*, but Nadine tries hard not to listen.

Have you read the reviews? Mia asks. Nadine doesn't know anything about any reviews. *No*, she says. *Don't*, Mia says, and chuckles, *those critics did not go easy on me. Okay then*, Nadine says, *I won't. Oh, I'm joking*, Mia says, *of course you can read them.* Nadine resists the urge to take Mia's hand as she says, *These are beautiful, Mia, they're all beautiful.* She feels a bit strange saying this, she doesn't mean to suggest she herself is beautiful, of course, but Mia is nodding now, closes her eyes, says, *I'm very happy to hear you say that.* There's a moment of silence before Mia says, *The critics are right, though, that's the worst part; I'm always reaching for something and not quite getting there.* What is Nadine supposed to say to that? Look at *you*, she wants to say. Dare to look at you, and maybe you'll get there. But she says nothing.

Outside the gallery they hug, and a car screeches and comes to a full stop for no apparent reason. For a moment they both look at the driver, then Nadine looks at Mia and shrugs, and the car is back on its way. They hug again, because it is easier than saying goodbye, and at the end of that hug Mia grabs Nadine's shoulders, looks straight into her eyes, says, *Thank you.* Nadine shakes her head and looks down.

Then there is nothing to do but for Mia to take her hands off Nadine's shoulders, and when she does there is a sensation between them, a balloon letting go of the air inside it. Nadine wants to stand there with that feeling a bit, but she knows that if she does the next thing that happens will be restlessness, Mia's restlessness. And she knows this: she needs to leave before the restlessness comes, or restlessness will be the last thing they ever share. *Goodbye, then*, Nadine says, and Mia says, *Bye*, and her eyes seem to tear up a bit, but Nadine isn't sure, it might be from the wind. And on that thought Nadine turns around and walks away, hoping that Mia is standing there looking at her. If she is, she is no doubt noticing the composition—the widening of the street toward the end of the block, the sprawling streetlights and brown skies, Nadine's back getting smaller—and she is squinting and gently biting her lip, regretting that she doesn't have her camera.

ACKNOWLEDGMENTS

I grew up in another language. For teaching me to write in English, for showing me how to be a person and a woman and a writer in New York—I'm indebted to more people than I could ever list here.

Elizabeth Reichert, this book is yours as much as it is mine.

PJ Mark, it has recently been scientifically proven, is the best literary agent on earth. Thank you, PJ, for believing in me so long before there was any real reason to. And thank you for saying "a book is born when it is ready to be born."

Emily Bell is a rockstar editor. Rumor has it some writers are now tattooing her name on their bodies. Thank you, Emily, for your skill and for your heart.

FSG is full of rockstars, and I am grateful to every single one of them, especially Jeff Seroy, who responds to e-mails before he receives them, and Brian Gittis, a magician in glasses.

A huge thank-you also goes out to everyone at Random House Canada, and mostly to Kiara Kent. Kiara, thank you for your generosity and your kindness and your intelligence.

My parents, Avi and Eliya Oria, and my sister, Dana Oria, are three of my most favorite people in this world, and they are the people I talk to when I forget how to breathe. Each of them is a powerhouse of strength and talent, and together they are an army.

My two years at the MFA writing program at Sarah Lawrence College taught me most of what I know as a writer. In my life, SLC has been a gift that keeps on giving, and I am forever grateful to everyone in that community.

The following humans helped tremendously with early versions of these stories and/or showed up for me in more ways than I can count: Melissa Febos, Nelly Reifler, Caitlin Delohery, Hossannah Asuncion, Diana Spechler, Joshua Henkin, Claire Oria-Friedman, Charlotte Oria, Jill Jarvis, Galit Lotan, Ryan Britt, Birna Anna Bjornsdottir, Aryn Kyle, Kate Angus, Alison Espach, Maya Michaeli, Asaf Sandhaus, Annie Levy, Tali Herskowitz, Julie Stevenson, Syreeta McFadden, Greg Blumstein, Manya Fox, Honor Moore.

Thank you, Ariel Steinlauf, for years of love and friendship, and for the title of this book.

Special thanks to T Kira Madden, Karissa Chen, and Chesley Hicks, for their talents and generosity.

Elizabeth Cohen, a gifted tourguide: thank you always.

Thank you, Aspen Matis, for writing alongside me on some tough days, and for lending me your bionic ear whenever I asked. And to everyone in the Joe community past and present: you people remind me why and show me how.

In the last few years, I've gotten to walk to a gorgeous campus in the middle of Brooklyn and talk about fiction for a living. Thank you for that, Thad Ziolkowski and everyone at Pratt, and thank you for your spirit.

If heaven exists it is the MacDowell Colony, and in the past couple of years I've been lucky enough to die twice. I don't know that I would ever have finished this collection without that good fortune.

I am similarly indebted to the Kimmel Harding Nelson Center for the Arts, the Sozopol Fiction Seminars in Bulgaria, the Writer's Room at the Betsy, and the Ucross Foundation.

This book is dedicated to Nehama Segalovitz. Writing is nothing more than a way to look for you.